THE
BAR MITZVAH
MURDER

THE
BAR MITZVAH
MURDER

A CHRISTINE BENNETT MYSTERY

LEE HARRIS

THORNDIKE
CHIVERS

This Large Print edition is published by Thorndike Press®, Waterville, Maine USA and by BBC Audiobooks, Ltd, Bath, England.

Published in 2004 in the U.S. by arrangement with Fawcett Books, a division of Random House, Inc.

Published in 2004 in the U.K. by arrangement with the author.

U.S. Hardcover 0-7862-6436-5 (Mystery)
U.K. Hardcover 0-7540-9651-3 (Chivers Large Print)
U.K. Softcover 0-7540-9652-1 (Camden Large Print)

The text of this Large Print edition is unabridged.
Other aspects of the book may vary from the original edition.

Set in 16 pt. Plantin by Christina S. Huff.

Printed in the United States on permanent paper.

British Library Cataloguing-in-Publication Data available

Library of Congress Cataloging-in-Publication Data
Harris, Lee, 1935–
    The Bar mitzvah murder : a Christine Bennett mystery / Lee Harris.
        p. cm.
    ISBN 0-7862-6436-5 (lg. print : hc : alk. paper)
    1. Bennett, Christine (Fictitious character) — Fiction.
2. Jews — Crimes against — Fiction.   3. Americans —
Jerusalem — Fiction.   4. Women detectives — Fiction.
5. Bar mitzvah — Fiction.   6. Jerusalem — Fiction.
7. Ex-nuns — Fiction.   8. Large type books.   I. Title.
PS3562.E23B37 2004
    813'.54—dc22   2004042501

For my sister, Edith,
who is always there

The author wishes to thank Ana M. Soler, James L. V. Wegman, and Dr. Edith B. Frankel for their information, their ideas, and their hard work.

And a special thank you to Lea and Dr. Raffi Frankel

Today I am a man!

What every Bar Mitzvah boy says
on his special day

PROLOGUE

I have more or less grown accustomed to change. While the biggest change in my life happened several years ago when I was thirty and was released from my vows as a Franciscan nun, the more recent changes have also had a great impact on me as well as on my family. When I met Jack, my husband of most of my secular years, he was a detective sergeant with NYPD, going to law school at night. Today he is both a lawyer and a recently appointed lieutenant, having passed his test with flying colors. He says that after law school everything else is easy. As I watched him study, I wasn't so sure that was true, but I'm glad he thinks so.

When Jack finished law school, he left the Sixty-fifth Precinct in Brooklyn, where he had worked for many years and where I had met him when I was researching a 1950 murder. At that point, he began the first of a couple of jobs at Police Headquarters, generally referred to as One PP for Police Plaza, more commonly known among cops as the

Puzzle Palace. But once he passed the lieutenant's test and received his promotion, commemorated by a big ceremony at One PP followed by a smaller one for the family in his office, a familiar cycle began again. He was transferred to a precinct following the rule from the Personnel Bureau that "new bosses of all ranks have to return to a uniform field command, a precinct, for at least six months after promotion." For various reasons Jack had thought he might get a pass on the rule, but it didn't happen and his life and therefore mine were turned upside down again. He began to work on rotating shifts. The chart, with its many changes and exceptions, can make family life very hectic.

I am a creature of habit and I like to sleep when it's dark and do everything else when it's light. Having a four-year-old just seemed to reinforce what I think of as a normal schedule. But crime doesn't adhere to any schedule and I suspect there's more of it in the dark hours than the light, so Jack psyched himself up and fell in step with four of these tours, then three of those followed by two days off, or was it three off? Talk about ships passing in the night.

A couple of days after Jack began the new assignment, someone called here at home and asked me if the boss was there. I was a little taken aback but realized he meant Jack. When Jack came home a little while later, I teased him about it.

"Yeah, I'm a boss," he said.

"OK, boss. Just checking."

I started calling him that now and then, and one afternoon Eddie asked when Daddy Boss was coming home. That really tickled Jack, and the name stuck for the duration of the assignment.

They were a tough six months for me and for Eddie, who couldn't figure out why Daddy was here one day but not the next, but I noticed something both interesting and amusing; Jack loved it. Yes, he complained about the shifts, but his spirits were high. He loves the action of a precinct, the interaction with the men and women on the job. He is really so well suited to that kind of life that I sometimes wonder what made him decide to get a law degree.

To add to his enjoyment, if you can call it that, he was assigned to what is officially Midtown South or MTS, as the cops in that precinct call it. It's over on West 35th Street and is billed as "the busiest police station house in the world." That's no exaggeration. It's always buzzing.

I was almost afraid he'd ask to stay on, but happily, when the six months were almost over, something unexpected came up. Although the commanding officer of the precinct, a full inspector, wanted to keep Jack there, just last week word came "from on high," as he told me, that he was wanted back in the Puzzle Palace. So he has begun the routine of cleaning out his desk and locker, something we've lived through twice before. What amazes me is the accumulation of stuff that finds its way home, only some of which is to be relocated in the new office. But coming from a family of pack rats, I'm the last one to voice criticism.

Tomorrow I'm going into the city to join the party at MTS and meet the cops Jack's been working with. And next week we all start sleeping through the night once again.

It was just at that point between the end of one assignment and the beginning of another when my friend across the street, Melanie Gross, called me somewhat breathlessly.

"Chris, you'll never believe what I'm going to tell you."

I laughed. "I must be talking to Mel."

"You are and I am. I just got home from school and took in the mail and found one of those quarter-inch-thick square envelopes on cream-colored paper hand-lettered by a calligrapher."

"A wedding invitation?"

"That's what I thought, but I was wrong. It's from Hal's cousin Gabe, a real sweetie who's made a bundle and gives half of it to charity. He got very interested in Judaism a few years ago and felt he hadn't been given a proper religious background. So he's having a Bar Mitzvah."

"His son is turning thirteen?" I said, recalling what I'd learned from Mel in a conversation some time ago.

"No, no, no. *He's* having the Bar Mitzvah. It's for him."

My head began swimming. "You told me a Bar Mitzvah was to mark a boy's passing to manhood at the age of thirteen."

"And that's what's usually done. But some men who think they didn't do it right, or maybe didn't do it at all, have one when they're older. And that's what Gabe is doing."

"So you get to go to a big party with lots of good food and all the relatives you haven't seen since the last Bar Mitzvah."

"Right. But Gabe is having this one in Jerusalem."

"Wow!" I said. "Will you and Hal go?"

"Gabe's flying us over and putting us up at a hotel."

"That's why you're breathless."

13

"That is exactly why I'm breathless. Can you believe it?"

"Honestly? No. That sounds like the extravagance to end all extravagances."

"But that's Gabe. He's very generous and he can afford to be."

"Mel, that is just stupendous. Are you taking the kids?"

"Chris, I haven't even called Hal yet to tell him. But why not? Even if they miss a couple of days of school, it'll be worth it for the experience. And I'll have to take off myself, won't I?" She said this last as though it had just occurred to her, which I guessed it had.

It was quite a story to tell Jack when he got home. He was as astounded as I at the expenditure involved but agreed it was a great opportunity for Mel and her family to visit the Holy Land.

Little did I know . . .

1

The party at Midtown South was a real pleasure for me. I had heard names and descriptions for six months, and now I matched them up with faces. One of the more artistically talented members of the precinct had written a short skit lampooning my husband, and when it was performed it had me rolling in the aisles. All in all, it was a fun afternoon and I was glad I'd been invited.

The following Monday, Jack got up at a normal hour, by which I mean the same one at which I normally arise, and had breakfast with us and went to his new office in the Legal Bureau at One PP, the car laden with cartons of stuff he could not live without. When he came home that evening he had some startling news.

"I found out today who it was that requested me for this new job," he said when we were comfortably ensconced in our usual places in the family room with cups of coffee and cookies, the paper, the TV, and a fire in the fireplace.

"It wasn't just some committee thing?"

"It came right from the desk of the Deputy Commissioner of Legal Matters and went directly to the PC's desk."

"Jack, the commissioner?"

"Himself. And then came straight down like a rocket, ensuring that the transfer would take place ASAP. The blessing of the chief of personnel came later. This was a non-stop transfer."

I put my cup down. "I'm not sure I understand."

"I'm not sure I understand, either. The captain told me today. Seems they want me for something special, but frankly, I don't have the vaguest."

"I hope it's interesting," I said, still spinning a bit from the mention of the police commissioner. It certainly sounded as though Jack had been noticed by people high up in the administration.

"Yeah, me, too. I hope they don't want me to write proposals or anything like that. I'd lose my mind."

Nothing happened for a week. Jack went to meetings, met people, found a chair that fit his bottom better than the first one, and that was it. In the meantime, I walked my new kindergartener to school each morning, finally agreeing to have him walk with

Mel's children, who, although a few years older than he, are good friends.

Mel and Hal accepted their great invitation, and Mel and her mother went out looking for a perfect dress for the event. Mel was just thrilled. She had never been to Israel, although her husband had gone there on a teen tour twenty years earlier, during which he scared his parents to death by never writing a single letter. This time, he told us with a grin, his mother was coming along and she could write all the cards she wanted.

Finally, in the second week of his assignment, Jack called in the afternoon. "You're not gonna believe this," he said.

I had heard that before. "Tell me."

"I just heard — oops, gotta go." And the phone slammed, leaving me in the dark.

I spent the rest of the day wondering what was going on. Had he learned what the Deputy Commissioner of Legal Matters had in mind for him or had his sister, the caterer, invented a mouthwatering new dish that would arrive by overnight mail at our doorstep? There was, of course, no way to find out till he came home, so I got dinner going at the usual time, handing out cookies and pretzels to Eddie and the friend he had brought home from kindergarten. Around five, Toby's mother came to collect her son and we chatted for only a few minutes, as we both had things to get done at this busy time of day.

Jack pulled into the driveway after six, came inside, and lifted his eager son off the floor. "How would you like to take a trip, my boy?" he asked with unusual excitement.

"To Grandma's?"

"Farther than that. How would you like to fly in an airplane?"

"Can we, Daddy? A real airplane?"

"Jack," I said, feeling as though I might be missing something here.

"Into the wild blue yonder, as my dad calls it. We are going on a big trip, folks."

The timer on my stove sounded urgently and I dashed to the kitchen to avert a disaster. What was that husband of mine talking about?

The husband in question came into the kitchen, kissed the side of my neck as I stirred my pasta, and said, "Eddie's gonna tell you."

"Tell me what?" I turned away from the stove and looked at a beaming Eddie.

"We're going to Grusalem," he said proudly, as though he really knew what he was saying.

"We're what? Jack, what is going on?"

"I'll explain it all later. Eddie and I need

18

some apple juice. Mind if I squeeze by you and get a couple of glasses?"

"Apple juice, glasses. What's going on here?"

Grinning like an idiot, he calmly removed two glasses from the cabinet, opened the refrigerator, took out the bottle of apple juice, and began pouring while I restrained myself from doing or saying something I would regret. It was clear he was relishing the moment.

"Dear wife, I have been handed the assignment to end all assignments. I am going to Jerusalem for two weeks."

"Jerusalem? NYPD is sending you to Israel? Have they lost their minds?"

He burst out laughing, nearly spilling apple juice on my reasonably clean floor, which would not have pleased me. Then he calmed himself and said, "I can't say anything too specific right now, but a decision was made to use a detective with a legal background instead of someone from a federal organization. This involves criminals that both the U.S. and Israel have an interest in bringing to justice. I'm not going out and hunting down these guys; I'll be working on setting up a database that both countries will use to track the criminals. They think I can do this in about two weeks."

I stared at him, catching my breath. Behind me, my pasta was going beyond al dente and on its way to mush, so I turned, took care of it, and looked back at Jack. "You're serious about this."

"Very serious. But you haven't heard the whole thing."

"There's more? They're sending you on a chartered plane?"

"I am taking my family with me."

"Us? You're taking Eddie and me?"

"When was our last vacation? If you can't remember, neither can I. This is perfect, Chris. They're putting me up in a hotel and it's OK if my wife stays with me."

"Jack —"

"Don't say anything. Just take it in and we'll talk about it later."

He knows me too well. He knew that I would be thinking of the complications of taking off from my job teaching a course in female mystery writers at a local college, that I would be thinking that Eddie shouldn't miss two weeks of kindergarten, that — He was right. I had to take it in and talk about it later.

"They're paying for the hotel?" I said, thinking that would be a huge expense.

"And all my meals. And some other things."

"I can't believe it."

"You look like you're about to cry."

"No, no, not at all. I'm just overwhelmed. We're going to the Holy Land. I can't believe this is happening."

"Well, believe it. It's a done deal."

The pasta was fine, the sauce was great — it's Mel's recipe, so it has to be great — and I had even learned to buy Parmesan cheese in a small block from a good cheese store and grate it fresh over the pasta. Eddie was a colorful mess when he had finished eating, so I got him bathed and off to bed, looking forward to the quiet time that Jack and I have learned to spend together in the evenings.

"How did this happen?" I asked finally. "Why you and why Israel?"

"I'm apolitical. I have no ax to grind. I have the right background — investigative — and I'm a lawyer. I've done a ton of criminal investigations and I know how to keep my mouth shut. I'm a natural for this."

"And you have a sparkling record that anyone on the job would envy."

He gave me a kiss. "Yeah, that, too."

"I notice you haven't told me much about the project."

"When I know what I can say, I'll tell you. For the time being, let's just say I'll have

plenty of work to do and a couple of week-
ends free when we can tour the country."

"Oh, Jack, it sounds just wonderful."

"One more thing. I called Mom this afternoon and told her. You know, the folks have
wanted to visit the Holy Land for as long as I
can remember. They're thinking of coming
the same two weeks we're there and Mom
offered to keep Eddie in their hotel room, so
you'll be pretty free."

"Oh, my." I shook my head. "It's all too
much. What are the dates?"

"They're not fixed yet. As soon as they
know, I'll know."

"And to think I woke up this morning and
thought it was just another day."

I must have spent the next two days calling everyone I knew to tell them our good
news. Mel was as ecstatic as I and said she
hoped our trips would overlap, but I had no
dates to give her. The second person I called
was Sister Joseph, my dearest friend and the
General Superior of St. Stephen's Convent,
where I spent fifteen years of my life, many
of them as a nun. It turned out she had a
couple of friends who were in Israel study-
ing or working and she promised to get their
addresses and phone numbers in case I had
time to talk to them.

It was a most propitious time to be traveling to Israel. Peace reigned in the region, tourists went back and forth with ease. Quite a while later, although I could not know it at the time, the intifada would start and we would not have considered such a trip. But at that moment in our lives and in the life of Israel, it was the perfect time to visit.

I could feel the excitement build. I lay awake the first night after Jack told me, just thinking of how lucky we were. I started to check the weather in Jerusalem each morning in the *New York Times*, finding that it was a good deal milder than here in New York State. Mel told me the people tended toward casual dress and recommended I take sandals and sneakers for everyday and maybe one pair of low heels for going out to dinner. Her parents have visited Israel several times and I value her mother's judgment on things like this, especially where clothes are concerned. I'm still not a fashion plate and despair of ever being one and I'm convinced I would never have bought myself a wedding gown without Mrs. Margulies's expert assistance.

Although it felt like weeks as the pressure built, it was only a few days till Jack came home with dates and information on where we were going to stay. He had let his parents know immediately so that they could book a flight. Ours was being handled by NYPD. We would leave on a Saturday in November, arriving on Sunday, and stay for two work-weeks, with an option to spend an extra few days at the end on vacation.

I called Mel, whose dates I couldn't re-member, and found that her cousin's Bar Mitzvah was scheduled for the day before our arrival. We would definitely share a week or more in Jerusalem.

The Grosses were staying in a large modern hotel in the central part of the city, while we were staying in an old hotel of some note, the American Colony Hotel. It was situated not far from the American con-sulate in its own little compound, Jack said, and it was a short drive from the main police station, where he would be working daily. NYPD was renting a car for us. I think my heart nearly stopped beating when I heard that. It would be ours evenings and week-ends for personal use.

Although it was still a month or more till our departure, I became very busy. We ap-plied for passports right away, including one for Eddie, who was joyous at the prospect of flying in a plane and seeing Grandma and Grandpa. I had to arrange for a substitute to take over my classes. Happily, I teach one long morning a week and, having done it before, I had lesson plans and assignments already made. I found a remarkable teacher in the English department who said he would really enjoy doing it, and that made me feel better about leaving my students.

Eddie's school was unhappy that he would miss two weeks of work, but they agreed it would be a good experience for him and we left it at that. When I was sure everything was set, I went out and bought a suitcase for Eddie of his very own, so he could stay with his grandparents without difficulty. He was so pleased to own his own suitcase, I was afraid he would take it to school.

Jack was somewhat reluctant to talk much about the project he would be involved in, but he told me a little. Apparently, there were fugitives hiding out in Israel whom we, the United States, wanted back for prosecution and whom the Israelis would be happy to get rid of. They were primarily Russian Jews who held joint nationality status, were part of the "Russian Mafia," and had enough money to buy substantial legal representation. Jack said his experience as a detective sergeant in Brooklyn had provided graphic evidence that these people were dangerous, ruthless, and smart. The interests of both the U.S. and Israeli law enforcement agencies would be served by sharing closely held information on these fugitives' activities. It surprised me that in such a small country this could be a problem, but apparently it was. Now, in the days before we left, Jack was researching these people in files in New York. The Israelis, he said, also had files with additional information that he would see when he got there.

The time finally passed and our suitcases got packed. The Grosses left two days before we did on a plane with about forty other people, including the Bar Mitzvah man himself. They would arrive a couple of days before the event and have time to acclimate themselves to the difference in time, about seven hours, before the weekend of festivities.

We ordered a limo to take us to JFK, and Eddie's eyes opened wide when it came. We drive fairly modest cars and this was bigger than anything he'd ever been in. At the airport, we checked our luggage, showed our passports, and passed easily through the security checkpoint after Jack had a ten-minute conversation with a short dark-haired man who seemed to be waiting for us. We met up with my in-laws and eventually boarded the plane. My heart was pounding. This was really happening; we were on our way to the Holy Land.

2

The plane came in over the Mediterranean Sea. At one moment, the blue water ended and land began. We were fairly low and could see tall buildings and small houses. In a few minutes, we had landed.

To say we were exhausted would not describe how we felt. It had been a long trip and I think all of us ached from sitting so long. We went to our respective hotels in separate taxis. Although it was daytime, Eddie was half-asleep and hardly knew with whom he was riding. We kissed one another good-bye and took off from the little airport.

My impression of the drive is hazy. I remember that at some point I became aware that we were ascending a hill and I remembered from my readings that Jerusalem is built on hills. Along the way there were war vehicles that our driver said were left over from a long-ago war. The signs were in English, Hebrew, and Arabic, so I could tell when we were passing Arab villages.

Toward the end of the drive, which lasted

less than an hour, we climbed more steeply, then got on a very wide street with several lanes in each direction. We were in Jerusalem and I began to wake up. As I watched, the driver turned, then turned again into the grounds of the hotel and stopped.

"It's beautiful, Jack," I said, looking at the greenery and appreciating the privacy of the location. He reached over and squeezed my hand. Then we got out.

Our first real look at Jerusalem was that night after we had slept several hours and awakened hungry. My in-laws called and said how excited they were to be there, in a fine hotel with every modern convenience and a roll-away bed for Eddie that he thought was the best bed he'd ever slept in. They decided to have a bite in the hotel and sleep for the rest of the night, or at least until their grandson awakened them.

We had found a message from a Jerusalem policeman when we arrived and Jack had called him and promised to call back when he was awake and more clearheaded. He did that as soon as we finished our family call. I showered while they had their conversation, and when I came out of the bathroom Jack was looking at a map of the city I had brought along.

29

"OK. The guy's name is Joshua Davidson and he'll be here in half an hour to give us a nighttime tour of the city."

"How wonderful. I hope we can get a bite at some point."

"I told him we were starving and he promised to join us for something to eat before our tour."

"I'll be dressed in a flash."

Officer Davidson, a rather handsome dark-haired young man who arrived in casual clothes, was driving a small car whose license plate had white numbers on red, identifying it as a police vehicle. Happily, it had four doors. Jack and I were waiting in the lobby of our beautiful hotel, having taken a quick look around. The hotel was built around a central open area that was a restaurant, and although I hadn't had my dinner yet, I was already looking forward to having breakfast there tomorrow.

"Good evening," the officer said in a deep voice as we met him at the door. "Mrs. Brooks, it's a pleasure to meet you. Lieutenant Brooks, a pleasure."

"Please call me Chris," I said.

He smiled but said nothing, and it struck me he might not feel comfortable calling me by my first name, as there was a difference in rank between him and Jack.

30

"Let me take you to dinner and then I'll show you the city." He opened the doors on the passenger side and Jack gave me the option of sitting in the front.

In a minute, we were on the road. Our guide and driver kept up a steady stream of narrative, which meant little to me as I had no idea where we were or how it related to our hotel or the rest of the city, but I listened attentively.

"Would you like a light meal or are you very hungry?" he asked.

"I'm hungry," Jack said from behind me.

"Good; so am I. Now, if you look over to the left" — and he was off again.

"Looks to me like you have no skyscrapers here," Jack said at a pause, "no steel-and-glass buildings."

"You're very observant, Lieutenant. All the buildings in this city are made of Jerusalem stone."

"That's amazing," I said. "All the same stone?"

"And all of it from the Jerusalem area. Of course the height and style of the buildings can vary, so they don't all look the same. Tomorrow you'll be able to see the color. Here's our restaurant." He made a sudden U-turn and parked his car.

We got out and went inside. Officer

Davidson exchanged a few words in Hebrew with an older man whom I took to be the owner, and we were taken to a table at the far wall. The restaurant was half empty and it had the look of a family place, making me feel quite comfortable. Menus were in Hebrew on the right side and English on the left. While I looked at my menu, I listened for the sound of English from people at other tables but heard none. Joshua made some suggestions and I gave them some thought.

"Chris isn't a very adventurous eater," Jack said. "I'll try anything, but Chris takes things kind of slow."

I ordered fish, but Jack asked Joshua what he would recommend and then ordered a lamb dish. But first a group of small dishes, each with a different food on it, came to the table.

"I thought you might like an assortment of Middle Eastern foods," Joshua said. "Here is some couscous; this is hummus," and he went on through the dishes, losing me pretty quickly.

Jack was delighted. He took a piece of pita and began sampling everything. I waited, then decided to plunge in myself.

"You gotta try this," Jack said.

It was what Joshua had called hummus

with an unpronounceable first sound. Gingerly I put some on a corner of the thin bread and tasted it. In a moment, I found myself smiling. "It's delicious," I said. "What is it?"

"Chickpeas and garlic and some olive oil. I promise it can't hurt you. And your husband seems to like it."

"Jack," I said, putting another small bit on the bread, "don't leave this country without getting the recipe."

The meal was wonderful and the tour afterward even better. We were driven by the Knesset, the Israeli Parliament, and up to the Israel Museum and the university, a high point where we got out of the car and looked out over the desert and the Dead Sea, although we couldn't see much of it in the dark. We were constantly driving up and down hills and Joshua reminded us that Jerusalem was built on hills. We drove by Yad Vashem, the memorial to the many people murdered during the Second World War, past the King David Hotel to the gates of the Old City, which I hoped to visit, and to the Mount of Olives, where Jesus looked down on the city. We got out and stood near a little church above the Garden of Gethsemane to do our viewing.

After much sightseeing, Joshua drove us to yet another building and stopped. "This is the national police headquarters, Lieutenant," he said, "where you will begin work at eight tomorrow morning. I will now show you how to drive from here to your hotel." With that, he turned around and started down the wide road nearby, pointing out landmarks in the dark. "And here," he said finally, "you turn left and" — the car moved across several lanes of thin traffic into what I recognized as the compound of the American Colony Hotel — "here you are where we started from. It's a very easy drive."

"Looks good," Jack said from the backseat. "I think I can do that."

"Your car will be delivered to the hotel at seven-thirty. I hope that will be all right. As you can see, it's a short drive and fairly straightforward."

"Absolutely. Chris, we can drive there together and you can have the car for yourself."

I felt my hands trembling. This city was not the grid that New York is. Without a compass, I would have no idea whether I was going north or south. "We'll talk about it upstairs," I said.

Joshua had driven into the unloading area in front of the hotel. "There's a very nice shop just across the way, Mrs. Brooks. You will have no difficulty spending money there, but don't accept the first price you're given. Bargain a little."

"Oh, dear."

"It's accepted practice. Think nothing of it. And a word of caution: if you take a taxi, make sure the driver puts the meter on."

I swallowed and smiled. "Thank you for a wonderful evening."

We stopped at the front desk and Jack asked for a wake-up call at six-thirty the next morning. I was happy we would be getting up early. I've always been an early riser and I wanted to pack as much as possible into the two weeks we were to be here.

"Mr. Brooks," the young man behind the counter said, "you had a caller a little while ago, not long after you went out."

"A phone call?"

"No, sir. A woman came and left you a message. One moment." He went into a file and pulled out an envelope. On the front was written: "John Brooks."

"Thanks," Jack said. He came over to me and tore the envelope open. "Let's see. Looks like it's for you."

"For me?" I took it and looked at the sheet of paper inside. "It's from Mel. Why would she come over instead of calling?" I began to read what looked like a hurriedly written message. "There's a problem. Let's go up and I'll call her. I've got her number and her room number."

Upstairs, I called her hotel, looking at my watch uncertainly. She had dropped this off a couple of hours ago and it was getting late. They put me through and I heard her phone ring once.

"Hello?" It was Mel's voice, but she sounded breathless.

"Mel, it's Chris. I'm sorry we missed you. We went out for dinner and a —"

"Chris, listen to me. Something's happened."

"Are you all right?"

"I'm fine. We're all fine. It's Gabe, Hal's cousin."

"What happened?"

"I don't know. No one will tell us anything. I don't know if he's dead or alive. The only thing I'm sure of is that he's missing."

3

"Calm down; calm down. Give me the phone." Jack had been pulling off his shoes as I repeated what I had just heard. He took the phone from me and started asking Mel questions, most of them starting with "wh." "Look," he said finally. "I know one cop in this city — he just took us out to dinner. I'll call him and see what he can find out. . . . Yeah. . . .Yeah. . . . OK. You bet." He hung up. "Shit," he said. "I don't have Joshua's phone number. Where's the phone book?"

I found it in the usual place, a drawer in the dresser, and handed it to him. He opened it and looked at me. "This is the phone book?"

"What's wrong?"

"It's in Hebrew. How am I supposed to find this guy's listing?"

I looked over his shoulder. It was like a bad dream. There was no English anywhere in the book. It was useless. "Let's go downstairs and ask them to help us."

"There have to be ten Joshua Davidsons in this town."

"Come on, Jack. Don't be defeatist. Let's go down. I'll do it. I've still got my shoes on." Without waiting for assent, I went down to the desk in the lobby and asked them to look up the number.

There were only two Joshua Davidsons listed in the book, and the young man agreed to call both. As usually happens, the first one didn't pan out, but the second one did. Joshua was just walking in the door when his wife answered the phone.

"Is something wrong?" he asked when I told him who I was.

"Someone we know has disappeared or been kidnapped in Jerusalem," I said, stretching the facts in the interest of brevity. "The family has been told nothing and they're very worried."

"If you give me the particulars, I can look into it for you."

"Hold on. I'll have them transfer the call to my husband. I'm down in the lobby."

As Jack picked up, I went back upstairs, thinking that this was not happening. This was a work and fun trip, a time to enjoy ourselves. We were in the Holy Land; I was eating Middle Eastern food and touring the city of Jerusalem at night. How was it possible that a disaster could intrude? How could Hal's cousin have died or been kidnapped on this very important day in his life?

I listened to Jack's description of the few facts he knew: the name of the victim, the location where the accident had happened, the circumstances of his being in Jerusalem. When Jack hung up, he sat and looked at me, shaking his head. He was in his stocking feet and he had wriggled out of his jacket, which lay where it had dropped on his bed.

"This is wild. Tell me again. This guy Gabe, he's the cousin who had the Bar Mitzvah?"

"That's the one."

"And he got himself hurt or killed or kidnapped."

"Did Mel tell you how it happened?" I asked.

"She doesn't know. They found him lying unconscious on the grass and a cousin who's a doctor tried to revive him but couldn't get him to wake up. They got someone to call an ambulance, and they came and took him away."

"Where's his wife?"

"That's one of several questions I didn't ask," Jack admitted.

"Did they take him to a hospital?"

"Presumably. Mel doesn't know which one because the name on the side of the ambulance was written in Hebrew letters and she was too stressed to try to figure them out. I guess she knows some Hebrew, at least more than we do."

"Are you telling me they don't know where Gabe was taken?" I asked.

"That's what she said. They've been trying to find him in hospitals all over the city this afternoon, but either they don't have his name right or there's a language misunderstanding or — I don't know what. He's missing."

"Did they try the morgue?"

"Joshua said he'll make some calls and get back to us tonight."

"You said they looked for him this afternoon. Then it didn't happen at the Bar Mitzvah."

Jack looked puzzled. "Mel said something about that. The ceremony was yesterday, she said. And there was some big dinner in the afternoon at a hotel. But something else was doing today, another party with music and dancing."

"That's a lot of celebrating," I said.

"Look, the guy has a ton of money. You fly a planeload of your best friends to Israel, you better entertain them right."

"I guess so."

"We may as well get ready for bed. If

Joshua calls, I'll take it. This is crazy, Chris."
He got up and went to the dresser, where I
had put my handbag and a couple of maps.
He opened the big map of the city and
studied the back of it. "There are half a
dozen hospitals in Jerusalem that are listed
here. It shouldn't take Joshua too long to
check them out."

"I'll brush my teeth while you baby-sit the
phone."

I had just fallen asleep when the phone
rang. I could tell from the conversation that
it was Joshua, and I could also tell that he
had not found the missing man.

"What about the ambulance?" Jack asked
at one point. "Somebody's got to have a
record of a call and a location that it went
to." He listened and listened. After a while,
he said good-bye. "You think I should call
Mel this late?" he asked, sitting on the bed
in the dark.

"You have to. She's probably waiting up to
hear."

He made the call and I got the gist of the
situation. Gabe was not registered at any
hospital in Jerusalem. Gabe's body was not
at the morgue. Gabe was not at his hotel.
Gabe was not at the last place he had been
seen alive.

"I don't like this, Chris," Jack said. He was lying down and talking to the ceiling.

"You can't disappear. A body can't disappear. The people in that ambulance know what happened."

"Joshua will check it out in the morning. I'm sure I'll see him at the police station. You gonna see Mel tomorrow?"

"I'll call her in the morning. I had hoped we could get together and see the city."

"Ask her all your questions. Take notes. We'll talk at dinner."

"OK, honey."

"I don't believe this is happening."

The car was delivered as promised just as we finished our first Israeli breakfast. I had actually eaten some herring from one of the many dishes offered and I was feeling game to try driving. One of the secrets of my life is that I have always driven a car with a manual shift. As I am very careful with money, it always made sense to drive a car that used as little gas as possible, and now finally I have found myself among the majority. Most people in this country also shifted. Jack had learned how to shift when he was a teenager and he had had plenty of practice driving my car, so we didn't need any special favors. I had studied the map during breakfast and determined that the drive to the police station was as easy as it had appeared last night.

Jack got in the driver's seat and pulled out of the compound to the main road, made a right turn, and we were on our way. By day the city looked completely different. I got a good look at the shop Joshua had told me about and I knew I would drop in when I had a moment. In the meantime, I looked happily at the blue sky and watched all the little cars speeding along the road.

"Joshua told me to look out for Israeli drivers. They're not as polite as New Yorkers."

That made me laugh. "As New Yorkers?"

"That's what he said. I guess we'll find out."

The drive was as short as it had been last night, and we reached the police station well before eight.

"You gonna be all right with the driving?"

I was scared to death but refused to show it. "Sure," I said. "How bad can it be?"

"Drive with Mel. Then at least one of you can look at the map and check the street signs."

We both got out and I walked around to the driver's side. Jack gave me a quick kiss and said, "I'll find out what I can. You do the same."

"Have fun at whatever you're doing."

He grinned. "That's the name of the game."

I watched till he was in the building, then got in the car and made my way slowly back to the hotel. I had a tough left turn to get into the compound, but I made it. The parking situation wasn't great, but I found a spot around the side of the hotel under a tree and left the car there. It was twenty-five after eight as I walked into the lobby and saw Mel.

"Oh, Chris, am I glad to see you," she said, getting up from a chair near a window. She came over and we hugged.

"Any word?"

"Nothing. I talked to Marnie — that's Gabe's wife — after Jack called last night. She's distraught; what can I tell you? I didn't want to call her this early, but I didn't want to miss you, so I came right over. Hal's with the kids. I'm so shook up I can't even remember where he's taking them."

"How 'bout a cup of coffee? We can sit and relax a little — it's still early — and you can tell me what you know. Jack is hoping this very nice police officer will find something out today. At the latest, I'll talk to Jack tonight."

"Coffee sounds good. This is a gorgeous

hotel, Chris. It's so old-world. We're in a splashy new one with a pool and all kinds of amenities, but I really like the feel of this one."

"Me, too." I smiled and led the way to the courtyard restaurant. It was a bit cool, but it was so lovely there, I thought it was better than sitting inside.

"I love it!" Mel sounded delighted. "How about here? There's a little sun. In fact, I think I'll take my coat off and let the sun warm me."

We ordered coffee and I pulled out my notebook and a pen. "We have to go over this carefully," I said. "I heard a little from you, a little from Jack, a little from Officer Davidson. I need to know everything you can tell me."

"OK." Mel sipped her coffee. "Saturday was the Bar Mitzvah. It was wonderful. It really moved me to tears, Chris. Here was this guy who'd devoted so much of his life to business and he decided to rededicate himself to his roots. We all flew over together, you know, but most of us planned to go home separately. Hal and I wanted to stay on, and a lot of the others did, too. We're all in the same hotel and Gabe is picking up the bill for as long as we stay. This guy is just so generous. Anyway, Saturday morning we had the Bar Mitzvah in a temple in Rehavia."

"What's that?"

"It's a part of Jerusalem settled by German Jews in the nineteen-thirties. Gabe was wonderful. He read from the Torah and translated into English so his family would know what he was talking about. Hal made an Aliyah."

"A what?"

"People are selected to come up and say a blessing before and after the Torah is read. It's called an Aliyah and it's an honor to be asked."

"OK. Go on. That was the actual Bar Mitzvah."

"Right. When it was over, we went to the King David Hotel for a really splendid buffet lunch. It was more like a dinner, if you want to know the truth. The table had the most wonderful dishes on it, ice sculptures, the whole thing. And it was delicious. We stayed for a couple of hours. There was champagne, live music, everything."

"And then?"

"It was late afternoon when we broke up. Hal and I wanted to walk because we were so stuffed, so my in-laws took the kids back to the hotel and we just walked around. Jerusalem is closed up on Saturday, you know."

"It's the sabbath."

"And nothing's open, just the hotels and maybe some little restaurants. But it's not a shopping day. Even the supermarkets are closed. So we had the pleasure of walking on empty streets, looking in windows, that kind of thing."

"What happened to Gabe?"

"I don't really know. We hugged him and kissed him after the meal and said we'd see him the next day."

"So the celebration continued for a second day," I said.

"Right. Gabe said he didn't want to overdo it and have an evening out after a big day, so he scheduled the final party for Sunday afternoon."

"And where was that?"

Mel had a map with her and she opened it on the table, folding it back to highlight a small portion. "We're here." She pointed. "The party was here somewhere." She opened the map and circled an area with her finger. It didn't mean much to me, as I had not yet come to terms with the geography of the city. "It's a lovely place. We had a champagne lunch on the patio, dancing, and we did a lot of singing. The weather was gorgeous, so we were outside."

"Anything unusual happen?"

"You mean before Gabe — ?"

"Before, yes."

"Nothing." She looked at me blankly. "Everything was normal. We were a bunch of friends and family having a good time."

"You said last night that Gabe had an accident."

"That's what we thought it was. I mean, what else could it have been?"

"How did it happen?"

"We were all having a good time. I remember hearing someone say, 'Where's Gabe? He can tell you.' But no alarms went off. I don't always know where Hal is at a party. Then I heard Marnie — Gabe's wife — say, 'Gabe? Gabe, where are you?' I remember I kind of looked around, but I didn't see him. A minute or two later, I heard someone scream."

"Who was it?"

"You know, I'm not sure. I thought at first it must be Marnie, but it could have been another woman. It was just a scream. We all stopped talking and people started running."

"Where?"

"Around the back, behind the little band. When they saw us running, they stopped playing. I didn't really see him at first. A lot of the others got to him before I did, but I could see his leg stretched out on the grass. Hal's cousin Leonard — he's an internist in New York — pushed through the crowd and dropped out of sight. I walked over and saw him leaning over Gabe, testing his pulse maybe. Gabe was lying flat on his back, eyes closed. There was a little bit of blood on his shirtsleeve, I think, so I assumed he'd cut himself or hurt himself on something. I really didn't know what to think, it was so surreal. Here we were having a good time and suddenly something terrible happens. I didn't really grasp it till later."

"What did the doctor do? What did he say?"

"Maybe he was giving him CPR; I'm not sure. Then he shouted, 'Get an ambulance.' "

"Who called the ambulance?"

Mel looked confused. "I don't know, but I'm not sure anyone at the party did. It came so soon, someone in the hotel must have called."

"So someone inside saw what happened."

"I'm sure a lot of people saw it. There were waiters bringing drinks and coffee and whatever."

"OK, so he got picked up by an ambulance. Did his wife go with him?"

"They wouldn't let her. I remember that.

49

She started to climb in the back, to be with him, and the attendants pushed her out. They said she could see him at the hospital."

"Did they say the name of the hospital?"

"Not that I heard. Not that Marnie heard. The ambulance took off and — I'm not sure what happened next. Marnie was in a terrible state. Someone went and got her a glass of ice water. Then Lenny, the doctor, said, 'Come on; let's get to the hospital and see what's going on.' I think that's when we all realized we didn't know what hospital Gabe went to."

"Jack looked up hospitals on my map," I said. "There are about half a dozen. Officer Davidson checked them all, or at least some of them, last night."

"Everyone goes to Hadassah Hospital," Mel said. "It's big and it has a fabulous reputation. I think we all just assumed that's where he was going."

"Did you call?"

"We had the concierge make the calls. When we found out Gabe wasn't at Hadassah — there are two branches and they had no record of being called out to our hotel — he tried some others. Then a few of us got in our cars and drove to Hadassah Hospital to talk to them in person." She shrugged. "Hal and I were there. We heard the conversations. They never heard of Gabe."

"Mel, I think the first thing we have to do is drive over to the place where the party was and find out what hospital they called. Then at least we know where to ask questions."

"Good idea. I've had enough coffee to hold me all day. Shall we?"

4

It was a truly magnificent place, with lots of glass to let the sun in, a huge lobby, potted palms, and fantastic floral displays. Mel found the concierge and we asked him about the call to the hospital. He had not been at work at that time, he said, so he turned us over to the maître d'. The maître d' didn't know what we were talking about and suggested we ask for the hotel manager.

We cooled our heels for a few minutes while someone searched for the manager. He arrived with a frown, a stocky man in a suit bought before he put on his last twenty pounds.

"Yes, ladies. How can I help you?"

We explained. He frowned. He asked us to sit while he made some calls. We didn't say much while we waited. Mel was too fidgety to sit, so she got up and wandered to some shop windows while I kept my eye on the door the manager had walked through, half expecting him to attempt a quick escape. Finally he came out, a sheet of paper in his hand.

"I have checked with the restaurants, with the people behind the desk, the concierge, the bellman, and even the housekeeping department. No one I spoke to called an ambulance yesterday or was asked to call an ambulance. I think you have made a mistake. Perhaps it was another hotel."

"It wasn't another hotel," Mel said with an uncharacteristic bite in her voice. "It was the party for Gabriel Gross. I'm sure you're aware of it."

"Ah, Mr. Gross. Yes, of course. You should have mentioned that."

"I did." She was quietly fuming.

"And Mr. Gross became ill?"

"He became ill," Mel said, her voice like a steel rod meant to pierce this man's innards. "An ambulance came and took him away. We do not know where he was taken. We have been trying to find him since yesterday afternoon."

"I see. I'm terribly sorry. I promise I will look into it for you. I have Mr. Gross's Jerusalem phone number here. I will call his wife if I learn anything. I am truly sorry. Good morning, ladies."

I nearly slapped my hand over Mel's

mouth to prevent her from saying what she was feeling. The little man waddled away.

"Let's talk to Gabe's wife," I said. "It's late enough that she's probably awake now."

"You drive. I'll navigate."

We had taken my car — that is, Jack's car — from the American Colony Hotel to this one, Mel having arrived by taxi. My nerves were a bit ragged from the drive and I was beginning to understand what Joshua Davidson meant when he said Israeli drivers weren't as polite as New Yorkers. But Mel was a very good navigator, checking out our route before we began so she had a good grasp on how to get there.

I stopped and called my in-laws, who were nearly on their way out to take a bus tour of the city. Eddie got on the phone and spoke with great excitement about where they were going and how good breakfast was. I guess grandparents are just the best people in the world.

We got to Mel's hotel about fifteen minutes later with no dents or scrapes, so I felt lucky. Inside, Mel used the house phone to call Marnie Gross's room.

"She said to come up. She's having her breakfast and she's dressed."

"How does she sound?"

"Terrible. I think she's crying in her

54

coffee. She hasn't heard anything from anyone."

We took the elevator up. This was as equally grand a hotel as the one we had just visited. As we ascended, Mel explained that the party yesterday had been at the other hotel because the facilities here hadn't been available yesterday.

We got out and walked down a short hall to Marnie Gross's door. She let us in and we sat in the extravagant sitting room of a beautiful suite. It was clear that Gabe had spared nothing.

A half-eaten breakfast was on a cart pushed against the wall. Marnie, a lovely-looking woman in spite of her red eyes and worn appearance, asked if we had learned anything.

"We learned there's no record of anyone at the other hotel having called an ambulance," I said.

"How is that possible? I saw it come; I saw the men put Gabe into it. And everyone else there saw it, too."

"It's possible the person who called isn't at the hotel today. Maybe one of the guests used a cell phone."

"I've talked to them all. The ambulance came so quickly after Lenny said we should call one that no one had time to

55

make a call. Someone inside must have seen Gabe lying there and made the call. I just want to know why the police aren't working on this. My husband is missing. He's sick or hurt or worse. How do we get them to move?"

I explained about Jack and that he was trying at his end but that he wanted me to gather as much information as possible. "Maybe we can just talk," I said, "you and Mel and I, try to put yesterday's events in order, try to figure out where people were when your husband got hurt."

"What difference does it make where we were?" she said with exasperation. "No one in our group did anything to Gabe. And I don't even know what happened to him. Did he have a heart attack? Did he fall and injure himself? I am just at my wits' end."

I could see that was true, and I felt for her. I didn't want to argue that one of their guests might have done Gabe some injury, so I ignored her comment. "Can you tell me how many people were at the party?" I asked, starting with a neutral question.

She let out her breath as though she had lost an appeal. "We were forty adults and I don't know how many children. Gabe would know."

"Are they all relatives?"

"Most of them. A few are friends. He has friends that he grew up with in New York, men he's still very close to. Two of them came with their wives."

"Do they work together?" I asked, thinking of the competitive nature of business.

"No. They went separate ways where business is concerned."

"Do you like them?"

"I love them. They're good and kind and their wives are lovely people. The way you're asking questions makes me think you suspect some kind of foul play."

"It's possible."

"I don't think so. I think he fell or became ill. There wasn't a mark on him."

"There was a little blood on his sleeve," Mel said.

"Gabe has a lot of nosebleeds. It's nothing. He's talked to the doctor about it."

"Did you get a good look at the ambulance attendants?"

She looked confused. "I was looking at my husband. I wasn't sure he was alive. I was terrified."

"Mel said you wanted to ride with him, but they wouldn't let you."

"That's right. I forgot about that."

"Did you get a look at the face of the man who told you you couldn't get in the ambulance?"

She stared at me. "Yes, I did. Round. Dark eyes. Small black beard. Sort of chubby, his shirt coming out of his pants. And he was wearing a *kippa*."

"What?"

"That's the little round hat Jewish men wear to temple and religious men wear all the time," Mel said.

"I see." I wrote down a phonetic rendering of the word, then turned to Marnie. "So you did get a good look at one of them."

"Yes, I did. I'm glad you asked. I hadn't remembered."

"Would you recognize him again?"

"I would. I'm sure of it."

"Good. If we don't learn anything, we can always go to all the hospitals and ask to look at their ambulance attendants."

"Yes," Marnie said, a look of almost relief spreading over her face. "Yes, we could do that. I would know him if I saw him again."

"OK. Now, if you don't mind, let's go over the guest list."

I had been lucky. When she realized she actually had a piece of important information, the identity of an ambulance attendant, she became more willing to talk about the people at the party. We went through them with Mel's help, as Marnie didn't have a list of names handy. Between them they came up with thirty-six of the adults, including the two old friends, Gabe's sister and brother, their parents, and a lot of cousins, all with spouses. We spent quite some time at it, and just as we were finishing up, the phone rang. Marnie jumped up to answer it, nearly stumbling on a purse left on the floor.

A minute later she looked at me and said, "I think this may be your husband."

It was. "How're you doin'?" he asked.

"Learning things but getting nowhere. What about you?"

"Joshua's very upset and embarrassed about this. He says it's been handled badly — tell me something I don't know — and he's gone to the two major hospitals to try to find out if Gabe is at one of them. He called in a few minutes ago and said Gabe is still missing."

"This is terrible."

"I know. Joshua's going to look into the morgue, too. He wants to know if it was really an ambulance that picked this man up."

"What else could it have been?"

"I don't know, maybe a bakery truck that saw a problem and picked him up and dropped him off at a hospital."

"Jack, you can't be serious."

"I am. Maybe some panel truck drove by, saw there was a problem, and decided to help. If they dropped him off and left, the hospital wouldn't know who he was if he was unconscious or dead."

"I'll ask."

"Meantime, there's nothing in police files that Joshua can find."

"Keep trying."

"You bet. Talk to you later."

I hung up and rejoined the women. "Jack suggested it might not have been an ambulance that picked your husband up."

"How is that possible?"

"Maybe a panel truck was passing by and saw something wrong and stopped to help. Since you don't know what was written on the side of the truck, it could have been anything." I had decided not to use Jack's example. "Or maybe someone from the hotel flagged them down."

"But they seemed so professional," Marnie said. "They knew what they were doing."

"And they had a gurney," Mel said.

"That's not my imagination. I saw it. It was one of those things that collapse to sit on the ground and then lift so they're about so high." She showed me with her hands.

Marnie agreed. "That's right. And they had the kinds of things you'd expect an ambulance to have. I started to get inside, so I'm sure."

Well, it had been a try. "OK. We're better off if it was an ambulance. There can only be so many in the city and we can track them down. Marnie, did your husband say anything to you? To anyone?"

She shook her head and grabbed a tissue. "He wasn't conscious. He was just lying there with his eyes closed, not moving." She started to cry. "I'm sorry. This is very painful."

I got up and found my purse. "Mel, I think we've done all we can right here. I'd really like to talk to the cousin who's a doctor, but otherwise, I think we should leave Marnie to take it easy."

"I disagree," Mel said, getting to her feet. "I think the three of us should go to the hospitals right now and see if Marnie can identify an ambulance attendant."

I looked at Marnie. She nodded. "Mel's right. Sitting in this room is just making me more depressed. I want to get out and do something. I want to make something happen."

"Then let's go," I said. "Mel, we need you to navigate."

She pulled out her map, opened it up, and got to work.

5

Hadassah Hospital was in the northeast section of the city on Mount Scopus, just before the Hebrew University. These were places I had looked forward to visiting as a tourist and I hoped that would still be possible, but it was out of the question right now. We parked and went inside, getting a bit of a runaround until Mel insisted very firmly that we had to see the ambulance drivers and attendants. The woman we were making our case to relented, finally, made a call, and a minute later a girl in her twenties appeared and showed us the way to where the ambulances waited for calls.

The attendants were sitting around talking, snacking, reading, and one seemed to be asleep. Marnie went over and looked at him first, shaking her head. He was clean-shaven and his hair was on the fair side.

We then looked at all the men one by one. Marnie said no to each. As we inspected them, an ambulance pulled in and the two attendants rushed to remove an old woman who appeared to be in very bad shape. Marnie went over, keeping out of their way, but I could see her shaking her head absently as she saw their faces.

We asked if anyone had been working yesterday and had not come in today and were told these were all the same people. We started back to the car.

"These ambulances look different," Mel said. "The one that took Gabe wasn't from this hospital."

We consulted the map. There were a couple of Arab hospitals listed, but Mel was sure the writing on the side of the ambulance had been Hebrew. Even I could tell the difference in the script, having seen signs in both languages. We tried another Jewish hospital but had no luck. Mel and I took Marnie back to her hotel and decided to have some lunch.

"I'll show you a great place," Mel said when we were in the car. "It's called Nachalat Shiva and there are lots of restaurants and some wonderful shops. You need to do something that's fun, Chris. This is your vacation."

I laughed. "Are you sure?"

"I'm positive. We'll have a leisurely lunch and then we'll go to some great stores. I hope we can park."

We were lucky. We parked in a lot that barely had room for us to move, but someone pulled out as we came in and that gave us a space. The unpronounceable place we were going to was a few steps away, and we picked a restaurant where we could sit outside. Although it was November, it was very mild, and I enjoyed sitting under the awning rather than indoors. People walked by and I watched them, telling myself again that I was five thousand miles away from home, that I was in the Holy Land. An occasional soldier walked by, armed with a gun that could be an Uzi, accompanied by a pretty young girl who clung to his arm. Love is the same everywhere.

"What are you smiling at?" Mel asked.

"That couple, the soldier and his girlfriend. They're very sweet."

"It *is* sweet. Let's order before I pass out. Hal and I had the hummus salad with mushrooms and hard-boiled egg here the other day and I can tell you it's out of this world."

"I had hummus last night for the first time in my life. That sounds like a good lunch."

"Sure you don't want tuna salad?" Mel teased.

"I'm positive. I'm trying to be cosmopolitan or worldly or whatever the current description is."

"Good." She signaled the waiter and ordered for both of us.

It was a wonderful lunch, and I enjoyed every morsel. As Jack and I were eating dinner with his parents and our son tonight, I expected we'd have a big meal, so this was just perfect.

While we ate, Mel recalled two of the four missing names of people at yesterday's party and gave me a small amount of information about them. "You want to know about Marnie?" she asked.

"I hate to ask, but yes, I'd like to know about her."

"I'm sure you've noticed she's on the young side."

"I've noticed."

"It's a second marriage. Gabe married in his twenties, had two kids, and the marriage broke up. It didn't happen quite as fast as I've said it. They were married about twenty years and their kids were in college. No one in the family knew there was trouble until one day Hal's mother called and said she'd heard from her sister-in-law that Gabe and Debby were separating. By the time we got the news, they weren't living together anymore."

"I see. So Marnie's a second wife."

"Yes, and a very good one. They go together very well. I really like her."

"That leaves me with a lot of questions, Mel. First off, I don't remember hearing the names of Gabe's children when we went over the party list."

"They didn't come."

I almost groaned. I was orphaned before my fifteenth birthday and I would have done anything to have a parent to live with and love. When I hear about these family splits, something in me seems to drop into a black pit. "Do you know why?" I asked.

"It was a horrible divorce, Chris. These two people who had loved each other, stayed together through hard times and into very good times, just grew to hate each other. They couldn't be in the same room for more than five minutes. Debby accused him of all sorts of things that may or may not have been true and Gabe said she didn't care enough about him to put a decent meal on the table when he was hungry. He was right, too. There were nights he came home to cornflakes. And maybe she was right. I don't know."

"So the children sided with her."

"They were in a terrible situation. They really had to make a choice. They were old enough that there was no custody involved, they could live anywhere, but they weren't really able yet to live by themselves, so they stayed with Debby and saw Gabe from time to time."

"So their sympathies were with the mother."

"And still are," Mel said, "from everything I've heard."

"Were they invited here?"

"Definitely. Gabe told us."

"But they didn't come."

"The son responded. The daughter didn't bother."

"It sounds ugly."

"It is." Mel looked at the check, which had been dropped off a few minutes earlier. "Down the middle?" she asked.

"Yes. That reminds me. I have to change some traveler's checks. And get these shekels fixed in my mind."

"Divide by four. That's what most of the shopkeepers do."

We each paid our share and stood. Across the narrow walking street the restaurant fronted on were several shops. I was interested in seeing the kinds of things available in this part of the world, so I thought shopping might be a nice idea. Also, I had accumulated quite a lot of information for Jack and wasn't sure where to go from here until I knew what, if anything, the police were doing. Without Gabe's whereabouts — or his body — it was hard to know whom to question and what to ask, although I did still want to talk to the doctor cousin.

"Stop thinking," Mel ordered. "We have better things to do for the afternoon. I'm going to show you some things that will knock your socks off."

"Sounds good to me."

6

I have never been a shopper for luxury goods. Having been a nun in my twenties and having lived at St. Stephen's for fifteen years, I learned frugality young and have never been able to give it up. Not that I think giving it up is a good thing to do. Jack had told me before we left the States that I should loosen up a bit, buy myself something wonderful, and consider it a gift from him. I'm sure he knows me well enough to realize I could never do that without his being right beside me and pushing me hard.

But looking in the shops at Nachalat Shiva with Mel, who had been taken there a few days ago by a relative, was a pleasure. There were shops filled with ceramics by Israeli artists and jewelry stores with beautiful silver chains of varying lengths. Some were machine-made and some handmade, which the prices and designs reflected.

After we visited several stores, Mel guided me through a narrow alley between two buildings, up some stone stairs, and into a shop filled with earrings, pins, and necklaces made from beads of semiprecious stones. Each one seemed to be more beautiful or more interesting than the last. Mel walked around collecting the ones she liked, occasionally replacing one that no longer enchanted her. The beads were of different sizes and shapes in colors that really grabbed me: purple, green, turquoise, black, white, and almost everything I've left out. There were bits of silver and gold interspersed, lengths that went from choker to halfway down my blouse.

"Mel, this was very unkind of you," I said. "There are so many and I like them all."

"So do I. Shall we fight over them?"

I laughed. "No, you take them all. I'll enjoy seeing them on you."

"You're not getting away that easy, lady. I was there when your wonderful husband ordered you to buy yourself a present."

"It wasn't exactly an order," I said, gulping.

She gave me her great grin. "I'm taking this one. I never thought of lavender and green together, but I love it. Hal will love it, too. Excuse me." She turned to the woman sitting at the desk near the door. "Can I look at earrings?"

I had a great time watching this play out.

There were drawers and drawers of earrings, a dizzying number. Mel had told me once that Jerusalem was the jewelry capital of the world — her mother had been here a few times — and she and Hal had saved their pennies to spend during the trip. I could see why. I had my eye on a necklace of blue and green beads, but I thought I would rather come back a second time to make a final decision.

"Are they gorgeous?" Mel said, holding her beads up to the light.

"They are. And those earrings, too. Mel, you'll have to go somewhere very special to wear them."

"You bet." She took her bounty to the desk and I walked around the room again by myself, thinking it had been a long time since I last indulged myself.

A few minutes later, we walked down the stone steps, Mel's boxes securely in her bag. She was glowing and I think I was, too. We found the car, settled up, and Mel guided us back to her hotel.

There was a small police car parked near the entrance and Mel said, "Uh-oh," as we got out of the car. She had asked me to come in while she looked for Lenny, the doctor who had tried to revive Gabe. Now she started running toward the entrance. I followed her into the lobby, where she grabbed a house phone and asked the operator for Marnie's room.

It wasn't a long conversation, but when Mel hung up she leaned against the shelf where the phones were, her forehead in her hand.

"What is it?" I said.

She took a breath that was half a sob, turned to me, and said, "They found him. Gabe. He's dead."

There were two policemen in Marnie's room and they would never have let us in except that one of them was Joshua Davidson.

"Mrs. Brooks," he said. "You've heard?"

"This is my friend Melanie Gross. She just talked to Mrs. Marnie Gross."

"Come with me, ladies."

We followed him past Marnie, who was crying on the sofa, the other policeman on a chair near her, to the large bedroom, and we sat in the small sitting area at one end.

Joshua spoke softly: "We received a call a little while ago, a body found in East Jerusalem. From Mrs. Gross's description of what her husband was wearing, it appears to be Gabriel Gross."

"Then he never went to a hospital," Mel said.

"Apparently not."

"We checked them out this morning. Marnie looked at every paramedic but couldn't identify the one she saw at the party yesterday."

"We don't know who picked him up and we don't know where he was taken before his body was disposed of, but we'll find out."

"I have some information you may want to read," I said, looking in my bag for my notebook. "I talked to Marnie Gross this morning and we visited the hotel where the party took place and talked to several people, including the manager."

"You did?" He seemed surprised.

"She's very good at this," Mel said, promoting my accomplishments. "Don't give him your notes," she said to me. "You'll never get them back. Let's get them Xeroxed and you can give him the copy."

Officer Davidson's eyes widened. He smiled and looked as though he didn't know what to say.

"That's a good idea," I said. "We'll find someone downstairs to copy them and we'll come back with the notes."

"Uh, thank you."

"Has the body been officially identified?"

"Not yet. Mrs. Gross will have to do that."

"Not alone," Mel said firmly. "Someone in the family must go with her. That's a terrible ordeal."

"I understand. We'll find a relative here in the hotel."

We went down to the first floor and got my notes copied. The copies weren't terribly clear, but I thought Mel was right, that if I gave away the original, I'd never get it back. When we were done, I said, "Maybe that doctor cousin could go with Marnie to identify the body. And maybe we could talk to him first."

"I'll call," Mel said.

When she got off the phone we took the elevator upstairs and found Cousin Lenny waiting for us at the bank of elevators. I was starting to think of Mel and Hal's relatives as mine and I was glad to find that Lenny was as kind and forthcoming as the cousins I had come to know and love in Oakwood.

"You're Chris," he said, giving me a firm handshake. "Come to my room. We can talk. I assume there's news."

Mel delivered it quickly, then suddenly began to cry. Being stalwart had served her well today, but this was a terrible turn of events. I put my arm around her and held her.

"It's so awful," she said. "How could this have happened?"

"We'll find out," Lenny said. "You gonna be all right?"

"Yes. But it won't be easy."

"That's our Mel. We'll have to help Marnie out all we can. I assume they'll take her somewhere to identify Gabe."

"They will."

"I'll go with her."

"She's talking to the police now," I said. "We can go down in a minute. I just want you to tell me what you observed yesterday at the party."

"Ah, you're the friend that solves the murders. Glad you're here now, Chris. The police have been no help whatever these last twenty-four hours. Maybe your input will move things along. Let's see. I heard Marnie scream. That must have been the first I knew something was wrong. I went along with the crowd and found Gabe lying around a corner from where we all were at our tables and on the patio dance floor. I found a pulse, but it was weak. I assumed it was a heart attack and began to give him CPR —"

"You asked to have an ambulance called," I interrupted.

"Yes. Probably when I saw him or when I got to him. It didn't take long for them to come. I had hardly begun the CPR when two attendants dashed over with a gurney."

"Did they seem to know what they were doing?"

"Why do you ask?"

"Because they didn't come from a hospital in Jerusalem. They were never called by anyone in the hotel that we could find, although I have to admit we haven't talked to the guests yet."

"I doubt one of the guests called. They'd need to know the number. They would have had to get help from the hotel staff inside. What you're saying is, you don't think anyone called an ambulance."

"That's right. But one showed up. Did you notice anything unusual about Gabe?"

"I didn't spend much time looking. He had a weak pulse and his breathing was shallow. I was trying to resuscitate him. I don't believe I did."

"Did you offer to go to the hospital with him?"

"Yes, but Marnie said she'd go in the ambulance. My wife and I were going for our car when I realized I didn't know where the ambulance was going. And no one else seemed to know, either. We dashed back to find out, but the ambulance was gone."

"Did he say anything, Lenny?" I asked. "Did you talk to him?"

"I talked to him, but he never responded. I told him who I was and assured him he'd be taken care of. You never know what the patient can hear and I wanted him to feel that he was going to be OK."

"Did you see the ambulance?"

"I walked over to it with the attendants. I saw it from behind. I never saw the inside of it. They had backed up so when they took off all you could see was the back, and I never walked around to the side. Where are you going with this?" He looked at both of us.

Mel answered, "I think we think Gabe may have been murdered."

"Quite an elaborate murder, if you're right. You gals have any idea what the motive would be?"

"I don't," I said, "but I didn't know him."

"I don't, either," Mel said, "and I *did* know him. All I can think of is that he had a nasty divorce."

"That was years ago, Mel. And Debby is well taken care of. I know there was a lot of animosity, but that's history."

"I wonder," I said. I looked at my watch. "I have to pick up my husband in a while and I want to give Officer Davidson these notes we copied. Let's go down to Marnie's room."

I gave Joshua the notes when we saw him, and he told us he was about ready to take Marnie to look at the body. Marnie was white as a ghost and unsteady on her feet. Lenny went over to help her and she grabbed him and cried and he tried to comfort her. I asked Joshua to route me to the police station where Jack was working, and he showed me on my map.

"We'll talk later," I said to Mel. I thanked Lenny and was on my way.

7

Jack walked outside a moment after I pulled up at the police station. I switched to the passenger seat with some relief and he got in and we took off.

"Pretty bad news," he said.

"Yes."

"What did you find out?"

I went over it briefly, my talk with Marnie and our trip to the hospitals.

"That was a good idea, checking out the paramedics before she forgot what the guy looked like."

"As it turns out, the police probably realized when they found the body that Gabe hadn't been taken anywhere legitimate."

"No matter. You got there at the right time. This is very nasty. Sure looks like a homicide to me."

"I hope it looks that way to the Jerusalem police."

"It does. Don't worry. They're on it now. You can probably step back and have a good time."

I smiled. A good time sounded like a very good idea. "Tell me about your day."

"Well, we're building a database and I'm learning a lot about international criminals. One PP called me three times this afternoon," he said, referring to his office at New York Police Headquarters. "I hope they don't expect me to stick around an extra six or seven hours till they go home so they can call me."

"I'm sure they don't."

"Don't be so sure." He gave me a squeeze. "I'm looking forward to seeing our son again. Hope he recognizes us with all the brainwashing my folks are giving him. We'll probably have to buy him back. Speaking of which, have you and Mel had time to look at the shops? Joshua said there are great jewelry stores in Jerusalem."

"We did, and Mel bought herself a fabulous necklace of semiprecious stones."

"And what about Christine Bennett Brooks? Did she manage to find a little something for herself?"

"Oh, Jack, you know how I am about spending money."

"Get something for yourself. It's an order. I'm going to be busy all day every day at this job or I'd try to sneak out and give you some moral support. I thought Mel would do that."

"She did, but . . . Well, I'll go back and look again."

There was a message from Jack's mother when we got to our hotel. They had found a restaurant they thought we would all enjoy. We joined them there and found Eddie excited to see us. He was wearing a rather fantastic hat his grandparents had bought him, one with a small solar panel on top of the head that powered a fan in the brim. It didn't work at night or in the dim light of the restaurant, but in the sun it was quite an attraction.

"This is a nice city," he said. "We went on a bus and saw everything."

"Did you get out and walk?" I asked.

"Uh-huh. We walked a lot."

"Well, you're very lucky your grandma and grandpa are here. You'll have a lot to tell your kindergarten when you get back."

"I took pictures, too." He had taken along a disposable camera.

"Pictures," I said. "I hope I get a chance to take some myself."

After we said good night, Jack and I went back to our hotel and sat on the patio with after-dinner drinks. He seemed as content as I had seen him, enthusiastic about what he was doing and where we were. It made me feel very good. I had watched him change from a detective sergeant with unruly hair to a better-dressed and more serious lieutenant with a law degree. This trip, this job, were the culmination of years of work, study, late nights, and doing two important things at one time and doing them well. I was truly proud of him.

"What are you thinking about?"

"How lucky we are to be here. You've really made it, Jack Brooks."

"Couldn't have done it without you, honey. Oh, I almost forgot. Joshua's wife knows a registered tour guide who's a Christian Arab. He can take you around the Old City."

"A private tour?"

"Ask Mel if she wants to join you, but yes, a private tour. I think you should do it. He'll show you all the sights and take you to some churches you might not see otherwise."

"It's the Holy Sepulchre I want to see most."

"I know. It's on his list. I talked to Rachel Davidson. Can I call her and say yes?"

"Sure. Is it very expensive?"

"*Chris.*"

I laughed. "Yes, thank you. I'll do it."

"You know what I've been thinking? Are

we the last Americans who don't own a computer?"

I put my glass of sherry down, startled by the question. "I didn't think we needed one. Arnold gave me the word processor so I could do his jobs. I didn't see why —"

"Well, I can give you a hundred reasons why. Eddie's turning five. I don't want him to be the only kid in the class that doesn't have access to a computer. And you know what? I have buddies I haven't seen for a long time that I could stay in touch with via e-mail. I bet you do, too."

"Then let's do it."

"Glad you agree." He took a last sip of his brandy and called the waiter over for the check. "Nice night," he said.

"It's beautiful."

"Let's go upstairs and make it even nicer."

There was a message from Mel. I called her back and talked to Hal for a few minutes. He had taken the kids to a lot of places and come home to hear Mel's story of our day.

"It's like a bad dream," he said.

I agreed.

"Gabe was the most generous, the kindest guy in the world."

"We'll figure it out, Hal."

84

"Here's Mel, wearing the greatest necklace I've ever seen."

I smiled. Mel and I were both lucky to have generous husbands.

"Chris. I did some sleuthing on my own. I hope you don't mind."

"I don't mind at all. I can't even imagine what you've done."

"Well, I had an idea. I decided to call some hotels and make some inquiries and I hit pay dirt. Gabe's daughter is in Jerusalem."

"What?"

"I tried our hotel first, although I didn't think either of his kids would be likely to stay here. They weren't. Then I called the hotel where the party was yesterday. There's a Judith Silverman registered. That's Judy's married name. She was married last June, but she's registered in her name only. How does that grab you?"

"It's making me dizzy. I'll see to it that Officer Davidson gets the word."

In the morning I drove Jack to the police station and took the car. He promised to call Mrs. Davidson to arrange for the tour of the Old City and to tell Joshua what Mel had learned. After I left Jack off, I drove to the hotel where the party had taken place on

Sunday. I used the house phone to call Judith Silverman, and while she was reticent, she agreed to talk to me in her room.

I had spoken to Mel and told her Judy might be more open with someone who wasn't a relative of her father, and Mel said she would wait in her room for my call after the interview. She also said she would love a tour for two through the Old City. I was delighted to have company.

Judy Silverman was in her twenties, dark-haired and dark-eyed, slim, and expensively dressed. I am never expensively dressed, but I have learned to tell the difference.

"Who exactly are you?" she asked as I walked in.

"Chris Bennett. I'm a friend of Melanie Gross."

"Hal's wife."

"Yes. We live on the same block in Oakwood and we've been friends for several years, since I moved into the house I inherited from my aunt."

"Go on." She seemed very serious, unsmiling. On her left hand was a large diamond ring and a slim white gold band. Her pantsuit was black, with a pale pink blouse showing in the vee of the collar. I couldn't tell whether the seriousness was her usual demeanor or I was making her nervous.

"Do you know that your father was taken ill on Sunday during the party?"

"I'm aware, yes."

"Were you at that party?"

"I chose not to go."

"Do you know what happened to your father after he was taken ill?"

"I don't follow you."

"Do you know how his illness turned out?"

"No. I don't have much to do with my father."

"Did he know you were here?"

She took a moment before she answered, as though she was composing her response. "I doubt it. It's a coincidence that I'm here at the same time. I had nothing to do with my father's party."

"Your father disappeared for about twenty-four hours," I said.

"Really. Perhaps he's tired of his present wife and he was looking for a little fun. I'm sure if you know where to look, you can find that kind of fun in Jerusalem."

I was taken aback by the tone of her voice, its cold harshness. "Your father's body was discovered yesterday afternoon in another part of the city."

She stared at me. "Are you telling me he's dead?"

"He's dead, yes. Your father is dead."

"I — I can't believe it. He was in very good health."

"He may have been. It appears to be a case of murder."

"That seems — it's hard to believe." She pressed a hand against her breast. "I'm sure there are lots more people in the States who'd like to kill him."

"What are you talking about?"

"My father is a cutthroat businessman. People like that have enemies. Miss Bennett, why are you telling me this? What are you doing here? Why should I believe anything you say?"

"I'm a friend of Melanie Gross."

"You told me that. What does that have to do with anything?"

"Mel called me when your father disappeared on Sunday. I got the message when my husband and I arrived in Israel. My husband is a New York City police lieutenant. I've done some amateur sleuthing in the last few years and turned up some killers. Mel asked me to see what I could find out about your father's death."

"You think he was murdered."

"It would appear he was."

"My God."

"Are any other members of your family

here with you? Your mother or your brother?"

"No. I'm joining my husband in London in a few days. I came here alone." She said it almost without thinking, as though her mind was elsewhere, but she sounded sincere. She looked up at me, as if recalling that I was there. "How did you find me? How did you know I was here?"

It was a question I would have preferred not to answer. "We started looking for Gabe's immediate family when we heard he was dead, just calling around to see if one of you might be in Jerusalem." I didn't want to say that Mel had done it. "We found you registered here."

The look she gave me showed she wasn't accepting what I said as the whole truth, although it was very close to that. "Does my mother know about my father?"

"Only if someone has called her. I don't even know where she lives."

"He's really dead?" she said.

"That's what the police said."

"It's funny, isn't it? We were so angry at him for what he did to my mother. I must have wished him dead a hundred times. Now you tell me it's happened and I feel — I don't know how I feel. Certainly not happy."

"I'm sure it'll take some time for you to

accept that it's happened. You can call the police and talk to them. Marnie went to identify him yesterday. I haven't seen her since." I stopped, and then, before she could say anything, I said, "Mrs. Silverman, why are you in Jerusalem now?"

"I — I wanted . . ." It was clear she had no answer. "If you want to know the truth, I wanted to see the party without being part of it. They're all my family. I just couldn't bring myself to be a guest."

Something about what she said and the way she said it had the ring of truth. "I can understand that," I said sympathetically.

"Well. Thank you for coming." Her voice had become brisk. She stood and offered her hand. "I'm sorry I wasn't very helpful. This is quite a shock. I'll have to make some phone calls now, if you don't mind."

"I understand." I shook her hand and went to the door. I could hear her bolt it as I stepped into the hallway.

8

I called Mel from a phone in the lobby and told her I was finished talking to Judy.

"When are we visiting the Old City?" she asked.

"Tomorrow, if the guide is available. I can call Jack later. It's Officer Davidson's wife who's arranging this."

"I can't wait. Want to do some more sightseeing today?"

"Is that a euphemism for shopping?" I asked, laughing.

"Uh, not exactly. I wouldn't mind some more shopping, but I'd really like to see the Israel Museum. Hal took the kids there and he wants to take them somewhere else today. He's having such a good time, I'm afraid he's going to give up his law practice and become a stay-at-home father. It'll be the end of our marriage."

"It'll wear off, Mel. But I'm definitely up for the museum."

"Good. Can you find your way to my hotel?"

"I'll be there in fifteen minutes."

The museum was spectacular, situated on a hill and reached by walking up more stairs than I could count. Along one side was the Billy Rose Sculpture Garden, which we decided to walk through on the way out. But before we even got near the main building, we detoured for a permanent exhibit, in its own wonderful low, dark building, of the Dead Sea Scrolls. I nearly had to pinch myself to believe that I was standing a few feet away from those documents. I started thinking of the way we use the word *old*. I know people who have an old house: it was built around the turn of the century. But here were artifacts that were two thousand years old. It was mind-boggling.

When we finished, we continued up the stairs to the main museum and decided to stop in the cafeteria for lunch. While we ate, I told Mel about my conversation with Judy Silverman.

"What you're telling me is that you believed her," Mel said.

"Let me just say that she sounded believable."

"But what was she doing there? She went all by herself, without her husband, stayed in the same hotel where she knew her father's big party would be. That's no coincidence."

"Of course it's not a coincidence. She's conflicted, Mel. She feels she's hated her father since he and her mother split up, but something in her wanted to be part of his celebration."

"You need a more suspicious nature, Chris. Judy Silverman wasn't there to share her father's celebration; she was there to observe it or check out what was going on. You didn't happen to look out her window, did you?"

"Good thought. No, I didn't. I should go back and see what the view is. You're suggesting she could watch the party from her room."

"And maybe send messages to someone who was out to hurt Gabe."

"That's a very frightening thought."

"Somebody killed him; let's not forget that."

"And it was done in a careful, well-planned way that required the use of a special vehicle, at least two conspirators —"

"And maybe more."

"I'll have to tell Officer Davidson to interview her."

"I think you should."

93

"Let's find a phone when you're finished with your salad."

Finding a phone was easy; getting to use one wasn't. It turned out you needed a phone card that could be bought at any post office. We just didn't happen to be in or near a post office. Mel, however, is resourceful. She found a security guard and explained our problem and he offered me the use of his cell phone, so I managed to make my call to Jack's phone. He started out by telling me that Mel and I were on for a tour of the Old City tomorrow. Raouf, our guide, would meet us at the American Colony Hotel at ten A.M. and drive us in his car.

"And what's new with you?" Jack asked.

"Mel and I have just had lunch at the Israel Museum. We saw the Dead Sea Scrolls, Jack. It's overwhelming."

"So's my work here. We'll have to come back for a second trip so I can see what you're seeing."

"You won't get an argument from me on that. We're about to look at more of the museum. It's much too big to do in one visit. I wanted to tell you that I talked to Judy Silverman, Gabe's daughter, and she claims she came to Israel by herself. She's meeting her husband in London in a few days."

"You believe her visit is innocent?"

"She sounds believable, but I can't swear that she's just here to catch a glimpse of her father."

"I'll tell Joshua. I'm sure he'll want to check it out for himself. He's out right now, but I think he's coming back soon."

"OK. Just wanted you to know."

"You picking me up?"

"Sure."

"See you then."

Mel was delighted that our tour was on. She had a list of places in the Old City that she wanted to see, including the shop of an Armenian potter. "He's got fabulous dishes and tiles and serving pieces," she said. "My aunt has a set of hors d'oeuvre plates that I'd like for myself. If it's not on the tour, we'll go there later."

"We'll make it part of the tour," I said. "Jack thinks we shouldn't be two women alone there. Just to be on the safe side."

"Sounds like Hal. OK. We'll play it safe."

We selected a couple of exhibits and finished up in the gift shop, where they had postcards and books and other interesting things to tempt one. We both left with little bags of goodies.

By this time, it was getting to be late afternoon and traffic was starting to look like rush hour in a busy city. I drove to Mel's hotel and had a cup of coffee with her and then went to the police station to pick up Jack.

He was a little later than he had been yesterday, so I sat and waited. When he finally walked out of the building, Joshua Davidson was with him. I got out of the car to say hello.

"I thank your wife very much for arranging this tour tomorrow," I said.

"I'm sure you'll enjoy it. He's an excellent guide and we've used his services many times. But I must talk to you for a moment."

"Is something wrong?"

"It's about this woman: Mrs. Silverman, Mr. Gross's daughter."

"Yes."

"I'm afraid she's left the country."

"Today? She said she was going to London in a few days to meet her husband."

"We checked the airlines and a Judith Silverman boarded a flight to Frankfurt earlier this afternoon."

"I see. Maybe she couldn't get on a London plane."

"Maybe she just wanted to get on the first plane out of Israel."

"Doesn't sound very good, does it? I'm sorry I didn't let you know sooner."

"I think she may have checked out of the

hotel as soon as you left her. We probably couldn't have stopped her even if we'd known."

I looked at Jack. "I guess I misjudged her."

"Look, you found her. That's what's important."

"She didn't happen to mention a hotel in London, did she?"

"She just said London."

"We'll find her." He smiled. "Thanks for your good work."

"Uh, before you go, I'm told she's newly married. It's possible she has an old passport with her. She might be using her maiden name, Gross."

"Good point." He told Jack he'd see him tomorrow and took off at a jog.

"I screwed up," I said. "I should have told him sooner. What a mess. Pretty soon all our suspects will have left the country."

"You're right; that's a problem. But I've got a bigger problem. I'm starving. Let's pick up Mom and Dad and that kid of ours and have something to eat."

9

"We're going to Masada tomorrow," Jack's mother said as we sat down at the table in the restaurant they had chosen.

"I wish I could go with you, but my friend Mel and I are taking a tour of the Old City."

"Oh, we'd love to do that. Too bad we didn't talk to you before we got our tickets."

"I'll get this guide's card and you can call him," I promised. "And you tell me how to get to Masada."

"It's a wonderful trip, Chris. We visit Masada in the morning before it gets too hot and then we get to swim in the Dead Sea in the afternoon."

"That sounds wonderful. It's full of salt, isn't it?"

"Oh, yes. You can't sink if you try. I'm glad you packed a bathing suit for Eddie."

"I'm going to swim in the Dead Sea," he announced. "Grandma says I can stand up and float."

"Well, hang on to Grandma anyway, OK?"

"And we're going to do the mud," she went on.

"What mud?"

"From the Dead Sea. It heals everything. I'm going to pack it on my achy knee. I've heard it really works."

"And I'm putting it on my shoulders and elbows," my father-in-law said. "May as well try everything."

Why not? I thought. It's all right here.

When we got back to the hotel, there was a message to call Officer Davidson.

"Well, she's disappeared," Jack said when he got off the phone.

"Judy Silverman?"

"Into thin air. She got as far as Frankfurt, there's no question about that, but the trail is cold from there. There's no telling where she is. She's not in any of the hotels they thought she might be in. She's got money, right?"

"Lots of it."

"So she's probably not in a bed-and-breakfast."

"I wouldn't think so. Unless she's trying to elude the police."

"Draw your own conclusions. She's gone."

I lay awake thinking about Judy Gross Silverman. Obviously, she had come to Jerusalem to be where her father was at his Bar Mitzvah. What her motivation was I couldn't be sure. That she was hurt because of her parents' divorce I had no doubt. But was it possible that she wanted him dead so much that she would participate in his murder?

I wished I had thought to look out her window. First thing in the morning I would dash over to her hotel and ask to see her room or at least a floor plan. While I could not imagine a young woman killing her own father with her own hand, I could see her organizing his murder, perhaps giving a signal from her window to someone on the patio.

It irked me that Judy had taken off after I left. She had said she had phone calls to make, and I had assumed she meant to her mother and brother, perhaps to her husband as well. But I saw now that the call or calls had been to an airline, or several airlines, until she got herself on the first plane out of the country. She knew the police would be right behind me and she didn't want to be questioned officially. I hadn't handled this well at all.

In the morning I drove Jack to work and then went from there to the hotel where the party had been. The manager Mel and I had spoken to on Monday was there and remembered me. I asked to see the suite Judy Silverman had stayed in. He checked the register, then took me upstairs. The suite was empty and looked exactly as I remembered it.

"I just want to look out the windows," I said.

The look of distaste seemed permanently fixed on his face, but he said nothing. Probably he thought it was better to indulge me than to talk to the police. I walked from window to window in the living room and then did the same in the bedroom. Every window overlooked the patio where Gabe had been found unconscious. Judy could have stood or sat at any one of them and watched the band off to the right and seen her father attacked farther back and to the left. If she hadn't taken part in his killing, she might well know who had.

Before I left, I asked the manager where I could buy a phone card. They were available at the hotel desk and also, he told me, at any post office. With one in my purse, I would be prepared if I needed to use a pay phone again.

Mel arrived a little before ten and we waited downstairs till Raouf arrived. He was just as Joshua had described him, a man in his thirties, dressed casually and wearing an official-looking badge that identified him as a professional guide. We all introduced ourselves and went outside to his car.

I didn't make much progress on the murder of Gabriel Gross that day, but I would not have traded the day for anything in the world. The Old City was simply wonderful. Raouf gave us lots of historical, geographical, and religious information as we walked, and I made notes on the map I carried to remind me where various sites were. For Mel I'm sure visiting the Western Wall was the highlight of the day. Men and women were separated there, as was customary among the Orthodox. She had already prepared a message, written on a small scrap of paper, which she stuck in a crack in the wall along with many others. The contents of the message were supposed to reach God. She suggested I write one myself, and I decided to do so, asking for God's blessings on my family. Mel never told me what she wrote in hers.

The wall is at one end of a huge open area where people walk or congregate. There were several tour groups there, and we could hear German and Japanese as we walked by. It's a stunning sight, the wall, the people praying, and above and beyond it the gold dome of the Dome of the Rock. But for me the great moment was standing on the site in the Church of the Holy Sepulchre where Jesus was buried. The site is enclosed in a small building within the great church. Raouf had told us in advance that hanging on the rear wall of the inner room was a painting of Mary. If the resident priest was not there, Raouf said, we could quickly pull the hinged picture away from the wall and touch the rock on the wall behind that was the last piece of the tomb of Jesus and then shut it immediately. We did this and were apparently the only ones there at that time who knew about it.

There were candles burning everywhere, and I lit my usual ones, in memory of my parents and Aunt Meg. How pleased they would be to know where I was today. And how sad that they had not lived to see it for themselves.

There was so much more — the Via Dolorosa, several stations of the cross, long, narrow covered streets through which Arab women walked in their long dresses with heads covered, hundreds of shops selling all kinds of things from the Mideast. Mel and I both bought saffron at a wonderful-smelling spice store so we could make paella when we returned. (Mel promised to show me how to do it.) The spices were all in open sacks and were scooped out and weighed to order. Besides smelling very fresh and pungent, they cost much less than we were accustomed to at home.

There were shops selling fine jewelry and shops selling less expensive jewelry. We found the Armenian potter's shop and went inside. It was a shop with a few small rooms, walls and floors of stone, and beautiful, colorful handmade pottery. Mel found the set of eight different plates that she had been looking for, and I got a wonderful bowl that we could use for fruit or salad or just leave on a table to look beautiful.

Raouf took us to churches with fine tile work on the floors and walls. He saw to it that aggressive shopkeepers kept their distance, and I realized I was glad we were accompanied by a man. Between twelve and one we stopped at an Arab-run restaurant for lunch. Mel and I ordered several small salads and shared them while Raouf selected his own fare. We treated him; I'm sure we didn't have to, but we appreciated him so much, it was hard to express.

By the time the tour was coming to an end, Mel and I had both acquired a number of small bags with pottery, olive wood carvings, spices, and some other things we would enjoy at home for a long time. The last place we visited was the Cardo. This ancient Roman street of shops a couple of stories below street level had been unearthed recently by archaeologists working over a period of years. Today these modern shops sold jewelry and interesting clothing, small embroidered bags, silk, and lace. When we reached the end, we were once again in sunlight. We had walked through all four quarters of the Old City, the Jewish, the Muslim, the Christian, and the Armenian. We had passed the Citadel, which Raouf suggested we visit at another time, and we had seen more than I could remember without prompting.

Raouf drove us to my hotel, and Mel and I sat in the courtyard over coffee and dessert and talked about what a wonderful day it had been.

"My cinnamon smells fantastic," Mel said, sticking her nose into a brown paper bag. "I wish I'd gotten more spices. But that's what I always say when it's too late."

"I'm looking forward to making paella. Jack and I had it once somewhere in New York and I remember how yellow the rice was. This has just been an incredible day."

"I've seen so many pictures of the wall.

It's hard to believe I've actually been there. You must feel the same way about your church."

"I do. I'll write a note to Joseph tonight and tell her. I hope she's able to visit here someday."

"What are you guys doing over the weekend?"

"Oh, Mel, they don't have weekends here. Everything closes early on Friday for the sabbath, but Sunday is a workday. I'm afraid all we'll have is Friday afternoon and Saturday. Jack wants to drive around and see some other parts of the country."

"It's a small country. You can do that."

"What are we going to do about Cousin Gabe?"

Mel shrugged. "I think we've done a lot, more probably than the police. I'd let them take it from here. Unless you have some ideas."

"I always have ideas. Think about Judy Silverman. What's going on there?"

"Chris, Judy didn't kill her father. She may not have liked the fact that he and Debby divorced and she may have sided with her mother and blamed her father, but she's no killer. She's twenty-four or -five, for heaven's sake. She's newly married. It doesn't make sense."

"Why did she run?"

"I don't know." Mel shook her head. "She was scared. She didn't want anyone to know she was there."

"Why?"

"She's embarrassed. Her mother would be furious. Look at it this way: Judy wanted to come, but her brother didn't and her mother hates Gabe. So she makes her own arrangements, sits in her room, and cries while the rest of us are having a good time downstairs."

"She could have watched at least part of what was going on from her suite. If she looked out her windows at the right time, she could have seen him fall or get pushed or whatever happened to him."

"Are they doing an autopsy?"

"Yesterday or today. Jack will probably know about it when I see him."

"You were saying: she could have seen what happened from her window. Did it occur to you to ask if she called the ambulance?"

"No, it didn't," I admitted. "But it wasn't an ambulance, Mel. No real ambulance came. It was some kind of scam. The men in that ambulance and the vehicle itself were both part of the scam. But you're right: I should have asked her if she made a call.

And I definitely should have looked out her windows while I was talking to her."

"You've done plenty. I wish the police had taken it seriously when we first called on Sunday. Not that it would have made a difference. They wouldn't have found him anyway."

"Maybe Judy's scared because she saw something," I said.

"You mean like a cousin that she loved did something to her father?"

"It's possible."

"The family didn't do this, Chris. You couldn't find a motive no matter how hard you looked."

"Judy said her father was a cutthroat businessman."

"That's her anger talking. Sure he was a tough guy in business. That's how he made so much money. But look what he's done with it. He's given away millions. Judy will turn up. I just don't know where. Or when."

It turned out that Mel and her family were planning an automobile tour of the country starting the next day. I decided to take the bus trip to Masada and the Dead Sea by myself on Thursday. It was an all-day tour with plenty of time in the afternoon for a dip in the Dead Sea and the mud packs my mother-in-law had described.

At dinner they could not stop talking about the mud, the salt formations, the water itself. Eddie had apparently indulged in a full-body mud pack, and when we got home I would see the pictures of him covered head to toe. Jack and I thought the whole thing was hilarious. Eddie, of course, wanted to do it all over again, but we dissuaded him. Grandma and Grandpa were going shopping tomorrow, and he would go to the stores with them. That left me alone with Masada, the mud, and the Dead Sea.

10

It was an extraordinary day. The bus left from the King David Hotel, which is in downtown Jerusalem. Even the bus trip itself was exciting, the almost constant descent of the land until you pass the sign that says SEA LEVEL. And then you continue to descend.

Along the way in dry riverbeds the Bedouins camp, some of them with Mercedes-Benzes outside their tents and aerials erected to support TV usage. It was rather different from what I had expected.

The desert crept up on us. First the green foliage began to dwindle. Then it all but disappeared and the terrain became largely sand. Then came the hills and mountains, nearly all of them home to caves. I watched in amazement as we passed opening after opening in the mountains. Most of them were so high and the terrain so steep, it would take sophisticated equipment to scale the surface. Having just seen the Dead Sea Scrolls, I wondered what other treasures, perhaps thousands of them, might be hidden in those caves. It was quite a fantasy.

The previous evening Jack had told me that the autopsy on Gabriel Gross had been completed. There was, apparently, only one place in Israel where autopsies were conducted, in Abu Kabir near the city of Jaffa, which is across the country on the Mediterranean Sea. Joshua Davidson had heard the results and come to Jack's office to talk to him about them.

Gabe had been pushed or had fallen so that there was a bloody mark on one side of his face, hence the blood Mel had noticed on Gabe's shirt. But more important, a drug had been injected in his arm and that accounted for his being unconscious. It also accounted for the slowed pulse rate and faint heartbeat Lenny had observed. From this information Jack and Joshua decided that the initial assault had not been meant to be deadly.

"You think they just wanted to knock him out so they could get him in the fake ambulance and take him somewhere?" I had asked Jack.

"That's the way it looks. Maybe they were planning to ask for a ransom."

"Then why didn't they?"

"Beats me. There sure wasn't any publicity about the event that might slow them down. It didn't hit the papers till he was found dead."

"So maybe it wasn't a ransom," I said. "What was the cause of death?"

"They beat him pretty bad."

"How awful."

"Who knows? Maybe they wanted the key to his hotel room so they could go in and steal his wife's jewelry."

"Wouldn't they be smart enough to put that in a safe, Jack?"

"Seems to me they would. Think about it. Maybe you'll come up with something."

So I thought about it as the bus made its way to Masada. On our left I could now see the Dead Sea, while the desert stretched off on the right. There was little traffic and it was a straight road. Finally, looking exactly like the pictures I'd seen, Masada rose from the sand, an impressive piece of rock with a flat top.

We got off the bus and took a cable car to the top, where we began our guided tour. Although the air was pleasantly warm, I felt a chill as I heard the description of the men, women, and children who heroically held out against the huge Roman army, how, in the end, they took their own lives to avoid being captured by the enemy. The tour was a moving experience.

Afterward, the bus took us to the place on the Dead Sea where we could swim. I had lunch by myself, choosing not to share conversation after the tour of Masada. The lunch was made just for me, a salad buffet with Middle Eastern food, including hummus, which was rapidly becoming my staple.

From there I found the lockers, changed into my bathing suit and the rubber slippers my mother-in-law insisted I wear, and walked down toward the beach. About a third of the way there, I found the mud barrels. There were also showers to clean it off and mirrors so that you could see yourself covered in black. The barrels of mud were huge, and I watched a couple of young men in their twenties scoop out handfuls of the black stuff and slather it on their bodies and faces so that in a few minutes I could not have told what color their skin was originally. When a spot was not covered, they would help each other. Finally, they took a good look at themselves in the full-length mirrors, waited a few minutes, and then stood under one of the many showerheads and let it all wash off.

Just so that I could say I had done it, I

took a handful myself and rubbed it on my legs, thinking how much Eddie must have enjoyed this experience yesterday. When I was wet and clean I saw the little shuttle heading toward the sea, and I hopped on when it stopped.

The sea was amazing. At the shore, formations of salt grew at the edge of the sandy beach, beautiful white glassy growths that were hard as rocks. I walked gingerly on a wooden dock leading into the sea and let myself down at the water. I was immediately glad I had worn the bathing shoes. I could feel the rocky bottom and knew my feet would be torn to shreds without protection. Carefully I made my way out to where people were bobbing in the water and finally lay back and floated with the others. It was something I will never forget, lying on the water and bouncing gently.

And that was my day, full of history, new sites, and unusual experiences. When I got back to the hotel I showered in fresh water and then dressed for dinner. There was nothing new in the Gabriel Gross case. His body had been released by the authorities and Marnie was preparing to take him home for burial. For the family members who were not yet returning to the States she would have a memorial service in a few weeks. Before leaving, she sat down with a police artist and had him draw the attendant she remembered from the fake ambulance. Jack gave me a copy of the sketch in case I had to show it to someone. Marnie had tried looking at photos but got nowhere.

"And none of the cops that looked at the drawing thought they recognized it," Jack said.

"Did Gabe have business in Israel?" I asked.

"I think they're looking into it. His name certainly hasn't come up in the database I'm working on. They've made some inquiries at Interpol, too. And got nowhere."

"Someone should read his will," I said.

"You still think it's the daughter?"

"I don't really think it's the daughter. I just think when a very wealthy man is murdered, you have to look at who benefits. I think I learned that from a police sergeant I once knew."

"Who's gotten old and cocky and turned into a lieutenant."

"That's the one." I gave him a hug.

"Lots of people benefit from his death, all the ones you'd expect. His children, his ex-wife to some extent from what we've been told, his current wife, and more charities than you can count. But all of those have been benefiting regularly by having him alive. His current wife has the use of several homes; she travels and stays in the best places; she owns what I'm told is fabulous jewelry and furs. She drives a couple of great cars. No motive there."

"Unless she has her eye on another guy."

"Well, that's always a possibility."

"What about the ex?"

"Nobody knows the details, but she has the house they lived in and there was a settlement in seven figures. At least that's what some of the cousins say."

"Maybe she went through it, Jack. Not everyone counts pennies."

"The way my wife does. True. Ex-wives have been known to spend a lot."

"Was Gabe at Judy's wedding?"

"That came up, yeah. He was there. Someone in the new family said she didn't really want him, but he was footing the bill, so she accepted it."

"Was Marnie there?"

"Don't know. It might be in the file."

"Did a relative write the will for him?"

"Good question, and the answer is no. He went to an outsider, someone who's not here now."

"Interesting. He didn't want his will leaked to the family."

"Can you blame him? Who needs that kind of thing making the gossip rounds?"

I agreed with him. This was a family that stuck together and very likely talked among themselves. "I don't know how I'm going to be able to contribute to this case," I said. "It's clear this was a very sophisticated operation, and no one seems to have any idea of a motive. Of the forty people that flew over, I've only talked to Mel and Marnie, and they don't seem to have a clue why this happened."

"And I've gone through the computer here. And Joshua has done his own canvassing. Something'll turn up. It always does. And by the way."

"What?"

"I've talked to the guy I report to. Since we don't observe the Jewish sabbath and we do observe our sabbath, they're going to let me take off Friday afternoon, Saturday, and Sunday as well."

"That's great, Jack. We'll be able to go somewhere."

"But I have to make up the Sundays with extra days at the end. They're really concerned that this could be too big a job for two weeks, and I agree with them."

"Fine. But it gives us two weekends."

"Right. Want to pull out a map and see where we want to go?"

I pulled out not only a map but also a book I had looked at in some detail before leaving the States. The Sea of Galilee was in the northern part of the country, slightly east of Jerusalem, and we could drive around the whole perimeter in a day while stopping at various places of interest. Jack agreed that would be a good thing to do. We could leave on Friday afternoon and come back on Sunday after mass and breakfast. In the afternoon, if there was any time left, I could take him to some of the shops Mel and I had visited. It would seem strange being in a large city that considered Sunday an ordinary business day, but those were the advantages of travel. Things were different.

We discussed whether we should borrow back our son and take him with us, but Jack decided we shouldn't. We had promised his parents two solid weeks of their grandson, and it wouldn't be fair to renege. This was his vacation with Grandma and Grandpa and we had been seeing him daily, more, I thought, so he wouldn't forget that we existed than to check up on his care, which was about as good as any child could get.

11

I stayed up that night packing our one small suitcase, looking at maps, and deciding where we would stay overnight. On Friday morning, I made a hotel reservation for two nights. I was very excited about our little trip, glad we would have a couple of days together, and thrilled that I would see places of great interest to me.

When we finished breakfast, I dropped Jack off, went directly to Mel's hotel, and called Lenny's room from the downstairs phone. No one answered, so I looked in on the breakfast crowd and saw him at a table with a woman I assumed to be his wife. As I made my way through the restaurant, he saw me and stood to greet me.

"Chris, this is my wife, Sharon. Come and join us for breakfast."

"Just a cup of coffee, thanks."

"I suppose you've heard everything we've heard."

"About the autopsy?"

"Yes. And Marnie is going home now that Gabe's body has been released."

"Nobody seems to have a clue why this happened," I said.

"This is a terrible business. The cousins and I have been talking about it non-stop. No one can figure it out."

"Lenny, your family is very close. I've known Mel for six or seven years now and I've met her parents and Hal's parents and once in a while someone in the family comes to visit or they go to visit a cousin. Gabe brought all of you here and put you up at a fabulous hotel because he loved all of you. Is someone in this group here under false pretenses?"

I watched him exchange a glance with his wife. "If there is, I don't know about it."

"You're right that it's a close-knit family, Chris," Sharon said. "When Lenny and I were first married, I thought he had a million cousins, because he was always talking about one or another, making plans for us to have dinner with them or visit them. If someone told me that one of these people murdered Gabe, I wouldn't be able to pick the killer."

"Did anyone ever borrow money from him?"

"I wouldn't know."

"It wouldn't matter," Lenny said. "Gabe helped people. It wasn't a question of lending money that he had to have back. He could afford not to be paid back. I don't think he'd make an issue of forcing a repayment. That said, I never heard of a loan in the family."

"This isn't about money," Sharon said firmly.

"What do you think it's about?"

"I wish I knew. It's too big to be about money. A lot of people were involved. A truck painted to look like an ambulance. It makes me dizzy thinking of all the planning that went into this murder."

It made me dizzy, too. "You know Gabe's daughter, Judy, left the country and hasn't been heard from."

"I know." Lenny took his glasses off and rubbed his eyes. "Judy didn't do this. I'm sure of it."

Obviously, I wasn't getting anywhere. "When Gabe and his first wife split up, did Gabe have a girlfriend?"

"I don't think so. Not at that time anyway."

"Then why were his children so angry at him? Why did they both side with the mother?"

"It's what kids do. Gabe and Debby hadn't been getting along for a couple of years. The impression I got is that they both wanted out. But it turned into a battle. Debby wanted more; Gabe didn't want to give more. He gave her plenty; I can tell you that."

"I hear Gabe's will was done by someone outside the family."

"That's what I heard. Do we have lawyers among the cousins? Sure we do. But one's a real estate lawyer; one's a constitutional lawyer. No one does estate law, except maybe in a very simple case. I wouldn't make much of that. Would you go to a doctor because he was your cousin?"

"I don't know. My only cousin, Gene, is retarded and would never become a doctor or a lawyer."

"A lot of people *don't* go to doctors in the family. And probably it's the same with lawyers. I didn't use a cousin for my will."

"OK." He had made his point. Perhaps I was carrying the idea of family too far. "Do you have any knowledge of what will happen to Gabe's assets? Like the business?"

"I know he wanted his son to work in the business, but there was that bad blood. He offered Judy a job, too, but I don't think she ever took it. That doesn't mean he didn't leave them a big interest in the business. I just don't know. This will all come out eventually."

I wasn't sure whether he really didn't know the details or he was just trying to put me off, but I wasn't learning anything from the discussion. "OK," I said, giving up. If Lenny knew anything, he wasn't going to tell me. I went through my usual end-of-an-interview patter, where he could reach me if he thought of anything. "How long are you both staying?" I said finally.

"We're leaving Sunday," Sharon said. "Those were our original plans."

"Have a good trip home. I hope we meet someday in happier circumstances."

They echoed my good wishes and I got up to go. I had the list of guests in my purse, but they were all strangers to me except for Lenny. I didn't have to pick up Jack for a few hours, so I thought I might as well talk to whoever happened to be around, not that I thought I would get any more out of the others than I had out of Lenny and Sharon.

I found a house phone and asked for the first person on the list, a woman named Barbara Abramawitz. There was no answer. I went to the next name, Susan Greene. This time a woman answered.

"Mrs. Greene, I'm a friend of Hal and Melanie Gross."

"Yes. Is anything wrong?"

"Everything's fine. I wondered if I could talk to you for a minute."

"Sure. Mind if I meet you downstairs? They haven't made our room up yet."

I told her where I'd be and went to wait for her. She came down about five minutes later, a forty-ish woman with a few extra pounds, wearing dark gray pants and a matching shirt and carrying a black sweater.

"Mrs. Greene?" I said.

"Yes. Hi. Why don't we sit over there? My husband's out for his morning walk and I'll be able to see him when he comes in."

We walked over to an arrangement of couches and comfortable chairs and sat.

"Mel mentioned you the other day when I saw her. You're trying to figure out what happened to Gabe."

"And not getting very far."

"Well, the police haven't done very well." She sounded annoyed. "It took them twenty-four hours to take us seriously."

"I know. How are you related to Gabe Gross?"

"I'm his cousin on his mother's side. I'm not a Gross. I'm a Morrison. That's his mother's maiden name."

"Did you know Gabe's first wife?"

"Sure. We all did. We went to the wedding. I was just a kid, but I remember it."

"I'm told there's a lot of anger in that relationship."

"What else? That's what happens when people divorce. And Gabe got married again. Debby hasn't."

"The children sided with her."

"She brought them up. What do you expect? My children would side with me, too. Not that anything like that is going to happen," she added.

"It seems to me that someone who was invited to the Bar Mitzvah must have killed him or arranged for the killing," I said.

"What — one of my cousins? You're crazy. Is that what Mel thinks?"

I stopped her before she could launch into a tirade. "No, Mel and I haven't really talked about that. What I meant was, this was a carefully planned murder. Whoever did it knew Gabe would be here, knew he would be at that particular hotel on Sunday afternoon, and made elaborate plans to kidnap him."

"Doesn't mean it's a relative." She spoke with great certainty. "It just means it was someone who knew where he'd be. Lots of people knew. You think he sat down at the phone and made the arrangements himself? Of course not. His secretary took care of that. Talk to her. She knew every step of his itinerary. Maybe she gave the information to someone. Maybe she sold it." She nodded her head once, indicating she had hit on something important.

"That's possible," I agreed. "And I assume the police in one place or another will follow up on that. I just thought maybe there was some problem in the family, someone who didn't get along with Gabe. Maybe a person who was angry enough to do this."

"Gabe wouldn't have invited anyone he didn't love and trust completely. And you know who you're talking about? My brothers and sisters and cousins and aunts, people I trust with my life. You're off base here. You can put every guest through the wringer, you won't find a killer. Ah, there's my husband." That was the end of the interview.

I decided to give up on the guests. Probably I would find very few of them in the hotel by this time of morning and those I did find would represent a point of view similar to Susan's. These were all relatives by blood or marriage and she was right: if there was bad blood, they wouldn't have been invited. I would have to figure out some other way of gathering information or let the police do the job.

12

It was a pleasure spending the afternoon in the car with Jack. To be truthful, what I liked best was not driving. Israeli men are aggressive drivers, and while you feel this a little in the city, it's even more prevalent on the open road. Jack is able to deal with the flashing lights urging you to move a lot better than I.

He had gotten directions from a policeman on how to get to the road we needed, and for most of the trip we drove north not far from the Jordanian border. I had seen Jordan across the Dead Sea on the trip to Masada; now we saw it closer at hand, but there was little to see except desert. I thought that someday I would like to return and visit Petra, the city carved out of stone. That would necessitate at least an overnight trip and would be better done when Jack was strictly on vacation, not just a weekend tourist.

In the meantime, we talked as we drove, looking at the sights, at Jordan off to the right, slowing for the occasional village.

"So what progress have you made?" Jack asked finally.

"Not much beyond the initial things we learned at the beginning of the week."

"When you were way ahead of the police."

"Right. Now I'm not sure I am anymore. I have no idea where Judy Silverman is or if she's involved in her father's death. I talked to the doctor this morning, and if he knows something he's keeping it to himself."

"Why would he do that?"

"I suppose because he doesn't want to implicate a relative."

"Sound conclusion, but I bet you don't think it's a relative."

"And I bet you do."

"Hey, they're not only dearest but nearest. Every one of them had access to Gabe, including the doctor."

"Jack, if one of those people hated Gabe, Gabe would have known it and he wouldn't have invited that person to the Bar Mitzvah."

"Maybe Gabe didn't know it."

"How could someone close to Gabe hate him enough to kill him and Gabe didn't know there was a problem?"

"Have you thought about the wife?" Jack always goes to the most obvious suspects first.

"She's devastated, Jack."

"And maybe before she married she did some professional acting and learned how to appear devastated."

"There's no motive."

"There's no motive that you know about. There's a lot of opportunity."

"Forty shots at opportunity," I said. "They all had access."

"But someone had ties to Jerusalem. Someone was able to get that truck set up to look like an ambulance, to get a couple of guys to play a part at the right moment."

"Gabe's secretary," I said.

"Was she at the Bar Mitzvah?"

"I don't think so. Mel and Marnie gave me thirty-eight of the forty guests' names and they were all relatives by blood or marriage. Maybe an old friend thrown in."

"The secretary didn't have to be here. She just had to know the contacts. Trust me: she had them. In her position, she's got a Rolodex you wouldn't believe."

"There's no motive," I said with a sigh.

"Well, let's start thinking of motives."

I looked out the window. "I can't see the Jordan River, but I know it has to be there."

"The guy who routed me said when we get up north we'll see where it comes out of the Sea of Galilee and on the other end we'll see where it goes in. It's not much more than a trickle, he said. Not the mighty torrent most people expect."

"The Jordan River," I said. "I wish Joseph were here. For that and a lot of other reasons."

Sister Joseph, the General Superior of St. Stephen's, was my spiritual director for all the years I lived there and has remained my best friend. In addition, she has a real nose for murder and has steered me in the right direction so many times, I wonder if I could have accomplished all that I have without her help.

"I'm afraid this is one time you'll have to do without, although you could call her and talk."

"Too expensive." I would be on my own this time. Come on, Kix, I said to myself, using the name my cousin gave me when we were kids and which the oldest of my friends still use when they see me. "Motives." I thought about it. What would Judy Silverman's motive be, since she's the only suspect who's disappeared? I can't think of one. What about Dr. Leonard Gross? I closed my eyes and tried to imagine this very nice man killing his cousin because of some bequest. It was just silly. "How about

Hal?" I said brightly, referring to one of our closest friends, Mel's husband.

"Hal didn't do it." Jack sounded about as final as he ever did, and a little annoyed besides.

"Well, that's how I feel about the others. You know what? We need to see the will. There may be all kinds of interesting things in it. Like maybe there's a bequest for Gabe's first wife and it turns out she's running out of money."

"Could be. Ex-wives are good suspects."

I smiled. "You think it's possible he left her something in his will?"

"Not out of the question. It may have been part of the divorce settlement."

"It's too complicated. I'll never figure this one out."

Jack patted my thigh. "Whoever's behind this didn't want him dead, Chris. At least not right away. If they had, they'd've killed him at the party. They had the chance. Instead of giving him something to knock him out, they could've given him something lethal. But they didn't. So what does that tell you?"

"They wanted something from him. The question is what."

"It sure wasn't the money he had in his wallet."

"Maybe they wanted to know something he knew, like where something was hidden, like a key to a vault. Or maybe they wanted the combination to a safe."

"Two good ideas. See, what I've been trying to figure out is whether they intended to kill him from the start or he didn't cooperate and they killed him in anger."

I thought about it. If he had a key on the key ring in his pocket and they took it from him, they'd have to hold him till the key was used, or he would see to it that they were picked up. The same thing would hold if it was a combination or a computer password. But once the safe was robbed, why should they hold him or kill him? They could phone the information to an accomplice in New York or some other place, and as soon as the safe was emptied they could let him go.

"They didn't have to kill him if all they wanted was that kind of information," I said. "You told me he'd been beaten. That's the kind of thing you do when a victim doesn't cooperate. I don't think they meant to kill him, Jack. They wanted something from him, they didn't get it, they tried to beat it out of him, and he died."

"I think I go along with that. I'm not sure Joshua does. He thinks they worked out this elaborate kidnapping for a couple of reasons. They couldn't get him alone long enough to kill him. They didn't want to use a gun because they're loud. They wanted a quiet killing. Gabe was always surrounded by the family, because they were going from one place to another together. At the Sunday party, the tables and chairs were in one place, the band was in another, the dance area was somewhere else. Joshua thinks Gabe left the crowd to tell the head-waiter it was time for the cake."

"But he never got to the headwaiter and someone was waiting for him."

"Something like that. They just needed him alone for half a minute."

"If all they wanted was to kill him, why does Joshua think he was beaten up? And why did they wait twenty-four hours to dump his body?"

"About the beating up, Joshua thinks someone with a lot of hate killed him, or ordered him killed. That accounts for the beating. Why they waited so long, well, maybe they just wanted him to die slowly. Maybe they drove around looking for a good place to dump him and couldn't find one right away."

I shook my head. "This was so carefully planned. They had to know in advance where they'd dump him. I bet they watched the place day and night to make sure it was safe."

"I agree with everything you've said. We have a certain mind-set; the Israeli police have another. Eventually we'll find out who's right."

I saw a sign at the side of the road and looked down at the map. "I think we're getting close. Let's leave the murder for later. We should be coming to a turn. Tiberias should be off to the left."

"We won't miss the turn. If we do, I think we'll find ourselves in the Sea of Galilee."

"I wonder what kind of mud they have at the bottom."

Jack laughed. "That mud must have been some experience. No salt here, I don't think. You're right. Here's where we go west."

We reached our hotel a little while later and carried in our suitcase. This was a great way to travel, I thought, a single suitcase and a small car. I pulled the confirmation number out of my purse and put it on the registration counter.

As Jack was signing us in, the man behind the counter said, "You are Lieutenant Brooks?"

"Yes. Who wants to know?"

"You received a phone call about an hour ago, sir. One moment."

Jack turned to me. "You didn't give my name with 'Lieutenant' in front of it, did you?"

"No."

"It must be Joshua. They'd better not want me back tonight."

"Here you are, sir." The man was very deferential, as though the title had made a difference.

Jack opened the envelope and looked in. "Let's go to our room first," he said. "Whatever it is, it can wait."

We went upstairs and found our room, a small, neat place with two beds. I opened the suitcase and took out the change of clothes. There weren't many hangers, but there were enough. I put Jack's shaving kit on the bathroom sink and went back into the bedroom. He was sitting on his bed. "It's from Joshua. He wants me to call him."

"You think there's a problem?"

"I hope not." He called the operator and had the call put through.

Joshua must have answered immediately, because the conversation got started right away. I didn't really follow it, although I was pretty sure it had nothing to do with Jack's project. I walked over to the door and looked at the notices posted on it. There was the usual map of the floor with fire exits

135

noted. What amazed me was the number of languages represented. After Hebrew and English, there were German, French, and what looked to me like Japanese. What a variety of tourists must come to this place, I thought.

"OK, got a little something for you," Jack said.

"They find the killer?"

"Nah. They just located your prime suspect."

I thought for a moment. "Judy Silverman?"

"The one and only."

"Where is she?"

"In London with her husband."

"I don't understand."

"Apparently, she stayed in Germany overnight the day she left Israel, then flew or drove to London a day or so later."

"I saw her on Tuesday, the day she left. Today's Friday. She told me she was meeting her husband in London 'in a few days.' Sounds like she was right on schedule. Did Joshua talk to her?"

"Apparently. She wasn't very forthcoming about where she was in Germany. She didn't fly out of Frankfurt, which is where she landed."

"What did she say?"

"That she had planned to meet her husband, that they were spending a few days in London, and that they would fly back to the States when they were ready. He said she sounded annoyed and probably was intentionally vague to be annoying."

"I can't blame her, Jack. She had the right to leave Israel whenever she wanted and she has no obligation to tell an Israeli cop what her travel plans are. I'm glad she surfaced. It means she's no more a suspect than all the sisters and the cousins and the aunts."

"But she was at the top of the list."

"True. And now she's not. I started with no suspects and it looks like I'm right back at the starting gate again."

"Hey, that's life. Let's see what dinner is around here."

After a very nice meal, we took a long walk, stopping at the edge of the sea. I knelt and touched the water, Jack holding my other arm so I wouldn't tip over. The water was cool even though the night air was pleasant.

"This is a wonderful trip," I said.

"I'm glad they gave me the weekend."

I stood and touched Jack's hand with the water. He put his arm around me. "You're a good person to travel with," he said. "You want to see everything and you don't complain."

"There's nothing to complain about." We started walking away from the sea.

"My imperturbable wife. Listen, I've been doing some thinking about this homicide. The Israeli cops don't have a clue where that ambulance is or who the guys are who were on it. They've talked to the relatives who are still in Jerusalem, but they missed some who went home right away. I don't know if they'll ever find who's behind the killing, but you've got your own way of doing things. Maybe you can sit down with Hal after the weekend, find out what he knows. I don't think he'll give you a runaround."

"OK. They're coming back Sunday, too. I'll give him a call."

"Getting cold. Let's go back to the hotel."

Saturday was an incredible day. We took a slow drive around the sea, talking about Jack's work on the database, which he was happy to have a break from this weekend. We stopped to see churches and the places where the Jordan River entered and left the sea and ate casually when we got hungry. We especially liked the Church of the Loaves and Fishes and decided to return Sunday morning for mass there.

The Jordan River was a muddy trickle where it entered the sea, and there wasn't much more than that where it came out, halfway around the sea, to continue its trip south. We took pictures, though. It was something we wanted to remember.

In the evening we looked at a map. Nazareth was off to the west, too far to attempt on Sunday. We decided to go to mass at the church on the Mount of the Beatitudes, where there was also a convent, and then visit another place someone in the hotel suggested, as it was more or less on our way back south. This was a very old synagogue, Bet-Alpha, dating back to the sixth century A.D. or, as they say in Israel, the Common Era. This synagogue was discovered in the 1920s and unearthed after that.

What was exceptionally beautiful was the mosaic work on the floor, which is covered with images of mammals and birds, Jewish religious objects, and designs. What surprised me the most was the zodiac, the months of the year, and the seasons. Apparently, there was a time when the Jews worshiped the zodiac. We walked around, looking at all the beautiful images, happy they had been found and preserved.

When we left, we headed back to Jerusalem.

13

As soon as we hit Jerusalem, we were lost. The road signs got us to the city, but apparently, either you know your way in the city or you do your best. I scrambled to find a street on the map and direct Jack, but I didn't do very well. Suddenly I saw something familiar.

"You know, we're near that unpronounceable place Mel and I went to the first day we shopped."

"Get me there."

"Yes, sir." I managed it and we parked the car and got out, stretching our legs for the first time in a couple of hours.

"Restaurants and jewelry," Jack said, looking around. "I'm not hungry."

"Neither am I."

"Let's buy you a present."

We looked in a few shops on the street level, then went up to the wonderful shop where Mel had made her purchases. The woman inside recognized me and gave us a smile.

"This is more like it," Jack said. "What do you like?"

"Almost everything," I said. "But let's not spend too much."

"Stop bossing me around. I'm the only boss in the family."

I laughed. I let Jack lead me around the room. He would pull a necklace off its stand and have me model it. Then another. Then another. He refused to let me look at a price tag. I stood in front of a mirror and tried on one after the other. Just as I thought I might have made up my mind, he would come over with something else that he liked.

"They're really beautiful," I said, finally accepting that one of them would be mine.

"I like the blues."

"So do I."

"Try this one again."

I tried it.

"Like it?"

"I love it."

"It's yours." He took it off me and went to the table to pay for it.

"That's one of my favorites," the woman said, putting it in a box that she tied with gold elastic. She turned to me. "You're going to love wearing it."

"I know. I'm so glad to have something so pretty."

As we walked down the stone steps, I felt wonderful. Jack seemed delighted with the purchase. Feeling very good, we went back to the hotel and called my in-laws.

On Monday morning I dropped Jack off as usual and then drove to the Grosses' hotel, observing that I was now able to do this without consulting a map or feeling nervous. Hal had agreed the night before to sit and talk to me while Mel kept the children busy. I had the distinct feeling Hal was ready to stop being a twenty-four-hour father now that he had done it for a full week.

As I drove to the hotel, I heard the distinctive sound of an Israeli siren. Pulling over to the curb, I watched an ambulance drive by, lights flashing. To my surprise, the word AMBULANCE was painted on the side of the vehicle in English as well as Hebrew.

I arrived at the hotel early and sat in the lobby to wait. Hal knew where to meet me and I wasn't in a hurry. I had brought a book with me, as it was a little too early to pick up an American newspaper. As I looked in my bag for it, a man's voice said, "This chair is free?"

I looked up. He was probably in his seventies and very round, especially his face, giving him a friendly look. "Yes. Please take it." As I said it, I wondered why he had chosen that particular chair. There were more empty seats than occupied ones around the room.

He let himself down carefully, as though moving with too great speed or energy might put his body in jeopardy. "Ah," he said as he landed on the cushion. "A good chair."

I smiled.

"You are with the Gross party?"

"A friend of mine is."

"A very sad thing, his death."

"Yes, it is." I wondered where this was going.

"I knew Mr. Gross."

"The man who died?"

"Gabriel, yes. And I knew his father before him."

"Who are you?" I asked. I didn't feel threatened, but I felt a little strange. This man had sought me out to talk to me.

"My name is Simon Kaplan. Don't ask me where I'm from. In a short conversation I don't have the time to name all the places."

"You've traveled a lot."

"I have lived a lot. I have almost died, but something saved me. More than once."

"You're a lucky man." I was curious to

know what the point of all this was, but I thought it would be a mistake to hurry him.

"You could say that. You are not a Jewish woman."

"No, I'm Catholic."

"Ah, Catholic. There are many wonderful things for Catholics to see in Israel."

"So I've found out."

"But you have a Jewish friend."

"I know many Jewish people. And Catholics and Protestants."

He nodded. "You were here last Sunday when Mr. Gross became ill?"

"No. I heard about it afterward."

"It was not an ambulance that took him away."

Suddenly I had a witness. "How do you know?"

"The size was wrong. The shape was wrong. It came without a siren."

"You saw it come, Mr. Kaplan?"

"I was walking back to the hotel — I like a walk after a big meal — and I just happened to see the truck parked about a block away from the hotel."

"Just parked on the street?"

"Yes, exactly. A man sat at the wheel. He had a little telephone in his hand. Of course, nowadays everyone has a little phone in his hand, so I didn't pay much attention. But

144

this man was listening to his phone, not saying anything, just listening, and then, like that, he put it down and started driving to the hotel. I stood and watched everything that happened."

"Wait a minute," I said, suddenly realizing something was wrong. "That didn't happen at this hotel."

"No, it happened where the Bar Mitzvah party was."

"How did you happen to be there?"

"That is the wrong question, my dear. I was staying at that hotel. That is why I was there. The question is, how do I happen to be here now?"

"What's the answer?" I was beginning to wonder if he was playing some kind of game.

"The answer is, I moved from that hotel to this one a few days ago."

"Why?"

"Murder makes me nervous." He smiled and his whole round face lit up. Even his glasses seemed to shine.

"It makes me nervous, too. Have you told the police what you saw?"

"I don't see how it would help them. They know by now that the ambulance was not an ambulance, that Gabriel Gross was not sick; he was attacked. What could my little bit of information contribute?"

"What else do you know?" I asked.

"Before I decide whether to answer, please tell me what your interest is in his death."

"I'm a good friend of one of Gabriel's cousins."

"I see. And you are interested in finding out who killed him."

"If I can. The police weren't much help after it happened. The family couldn't convince them that he was missing."

"One hears such stories."

"What made you come to me?" I asked.

"I have seen you here, talking to members of the Gross party. I have overheard bits of conversations."

I had interviewed Susan Greene down here, I remembered. And I had sat at Lenny's table at breakfast time. It was possible that this little man had been nearby both times and I had not seen him. But the whole situation made me uneasy. He had watched me; he had sought me out. It flickered through my mind that I might be in some danger, although I usually discount that possibility with older people.

"Are you here to help me?" I asked.

"I, also, would like to find the killer of Gabriel. A man in the prime of his life should not die so others may benefit."

"Who will benefit from his death?"

"Many people. The obvious ones, of course — his wife, his children, the woman he was married to many years ago." He stopped speaking, almost abruptly.

"Perhaps they might have benefited more if he had lived another twenty or thirty years," I suggested.

"That is the long view. Many people nowadays have no patience. They cannot see beyond tomorrow. These people can be dangerous."

"Will you benefit from his death?" I asked.

"I? That is a somewhat impertinent question."

"You chose to sit here, Mr. Kaplan."

"I did, yes. Hmm." He sat nodding slightly, as though formulating a response. "No, I will not benefit from Gabriel's death. I have been retired many years now. I am too old to be mentioned in anyone's will and I have no financial interest in any company at the moment. I benefit from the lives of good people. Gabriel's life was a good one. I feel diminished by his death. You have read the poet John Donne?"

"I have. Many times."

" 'Every man's death diminishes me.' Do you believe that?"

"I do."

"We have all lost. Everyone." He looked down at his lap.

"Do you know who killed him, Mr. Kaplan?" I asked.

"If only I did. I would like to bring those people to justice."

"What *do* you know?" I had the feeling we might sit here for hours talking about poetry, about good and evil, and getting nowhere.

"I know the driver of the 'ambulance' was waiting for a signal. I know the direction in which the truck left the hotel. Ah, someone is looking for you?"

I turned to see Hal approaching. "Yes, but please continue."

"What is your name, my dear?"

"Christine Bennett," I said, using the name I generally gave.

"And you are staying at this hotel?"

"I'm at the American Colony Hotel."

"Of course. A lovely place. We will speak again." He raised himself from the chair, bowed his head deferentially in my direction, and took off.

"Chris, hi. Sorry I'm late." Hal shook my hand.

"This is very weird," I said. "That little man claims to have seen the ambulance pull up at the hotel where the party was last week. He's rather garrulous and I don't know if he knows anything useful, but he sought me out to talk to me."

"He's not a relative."

"No, but he claims to have known Gabe and also Gabe's father."

"Interesting. Maybe you'll run into him again."

"Well, let's get started."

"OK. I've made some notes about Gabe. I don't know if they'll be useful, but just in case. Where do you want to begin?"

I flipped open my notebook. "Gabe was older than you, wasn't he?"

"Quite a bit. He's in his fifties. He used to tell me he remembered the day I was born because my father called his father to tell him. I just remember him from all the family get-togethers. Gabe was always a lot of fun. He was smart, he could tell great stories, and he always wanted to have a good time."

"Were you at his first wedding?"

"Yeah. In fact, I think it may have been the first wedding I ever attended. I sat at the children's table with a lot of cousins at the dinner after the ceremony. It was a great wedding. Gabe was in his twenties, early twenties, I think, and Debby wore a dress that had all the women gasping. It was huge, billowing. I've never seen anything like it since."

"Where did Gabe go to school, Hal?"

"University of Rochester. I couldn't remember, so I called his brother last night. Gabe was a good student."

"And after he graduated?"

"He took some time off, traveled in Europe. His father didn't want him to, said he'd never get a job, but Gabe insisted and finally my uncle gave in. Gabe was gone about six months or so. He hitchhiked all over, fell in love with a cute little Dane, but decided not to do anything about it."

"What do you mean by that?"

"My uncle would have killed him if he'd married her."

"I see."

"So he came back and went to work for my uncle."

"What kind of work was that?"

"I think at first my uncle made parts for machinery. I know he had a lot of government contracts. He made Gabe learn the business from the bottom up. By the time he'd been there a year or two, he knew as much as his father, and he had some pretty good ideas to contribute."

"Did Gabe take over the business?"

"When his father retired, yes. But he moved it in a different direction. He started subcontracting a lot of work and opened factories outside the United States. It really became a global business. And it took in a lot more money than my uncle ever dreamed of," he added.

"Gabe has a son," I said. "Did he go into the business, too?"

"You know, when he was a kid, he worked there summers. I think Gabe hoped he could do for Barry what his father had done for him. The divorce kind of put an end to all that."

"They were really estranged."

"Yeah, they really were."

I flipped a page. "Tell me about Marnie."

Hal smiled a little. "Marnie is exactly what she seems to be, Gabe's second, much younger wife. If you're about to ask if she broke up the first marriage, the answer is no. He met her some time after he moved out of the house he owned with Debby."

"Maybe there was another woman in between?" I suggested. I still didn't have a motive and I was looking wherever there might be one.

"Chris, if Gabe had a girlfriend on the side when he was living with Debby, he kept it to himself. I never heard a whiff of a rumor that he was carrying on, as my mother likes to say, with anyone. Sure there could have been someone, but he was discreet. More likely, he and Debby just had problems they couldn't cope with and they split up because of them."

I have always been intrigued by the notion of problems that arise between married couples. We all go into marriage believing it's forever, promising that it will be forever. And then things happen. Jack and I have both changed so much since the day we met at the Sixty-fifth Precinct in Brooklyn back when we were thirty years old that I sometimes find it a little amazing that we have both adjusted so well to the changes in ourselves and each other. Perhaps it's just that we're both so busy we haven't had time to notice.

"Can you put your finger on the problems?" I asked. "Is it possible Debby was having a fling?"

"Interesting question." Hal leaned back and considered it. "Gabe did a fair amount of traveling, it's true. That's often when these things happen. But again, I have to say there was no family gossip."

"Debby wouldn't have leaked it to your family," I reminded him. "It would have been her family that heard about it."

"Right. I forget there are two families involved in a marriage, his and hers. OK, it could have happened that way. But I don't know anything about that." There was a certain sound of appeasing me in his voice.

"Just trying to look everywhere," I said. "Getting back to Marnie for a minute. Wives and ex-wives always seem to be the best suspects in a case like this."

Hal laughed. "More like husbands and ex-husbands, but I suppose I can make the leap. You want to know if Marnie's capable of doing what happened to Gabe? I can't for the life of me think why she'd want to. If they were having problems, I didn't hear about them. I think Gabe was crazy about her. She had some kind of job in public relations when they met, but she gave it up when they got married. She wanted to travel with Gabe; she wanted to be there for him. Did you see her last week?"

"I did. Mel and I talked to her. She seemed devastated."

"She *was* devastated. I know I've gotten rid of your prime suspects here, but that's the truth. Marnie was as crazy about him as he was about her. They were a great couple. They were planning —"

"Hal? Chris?"

I looked up and saw Mel coming across the lobby, her children in her wake. "Hi, Sari. Hi, Noah. How are you doing? Having a good time in Israel?"

153

They started talking at once, but Mel shushed them.

"Lenny got a call from Marnie late last night. She's been home for several days, but she had so much to do, she never got around to calling until now."

"What happened?" Hal asked.

"Something weird. Looks like her house was broken into while she was gone. Or at least the security system was turned off. You guys think it's relevant?"

14

As soon as Mel's words registered in my brain, I said, "Of course it's relevant. Do the Israeli police know?"

"Can't say for sure. I just ran into Lenny and that's all he told me."

"Someone disengaged the security system?" Hal asked.

"That's what it looked like to Marnie. She didn't go home right away when she got back to New York. Her sister picked her up and took her to her place. She had a funeral to arrange and all that stuff. Anyway, when she got back to the house, the alarm system wasn't working right and she finally got around to calling the security people yesterday. At least, that's what Lenny said."

"What's missing?" Hal asked.

Mel shrugged. "Maybe we should call Marnie. All this secondhand information is suspect."

I agreed. "Let's give her a call at home when it's afternoon there."

"She'll be sitting shiva this afternoon, I would think."

"Sitting shiva," I repeated. "That's staying at home and accepting condolences after someone dies. I remember when your grandfather died and the family did that."

"Right. They do it for seven days. *Shiva* means 'seven.' It isn't always seven days anymore and they don't sit on wooden crates the way my grandfather used to."

"You can't get wooden crates," Hal put in. "They don't make them."

"Right. So sometimes they print cartons to look like wooden crates on the theory that it's the thought that counts."

"Are you telling me they're supposed to be uncomfortable?"

"That's the point," Hal said. "To remind you it's a sad time. There are other things, too. You cover the mirrors in the house —"

"The mirrors?" I asked.

Mel smiled. "I remember when you told me about the mirrors in your aunt's house."

"How interesting," I said. "I had no idea." I had visited my aunt once a month while I was a nun and she arranged to cover the mirrors while I was there, as we were not allowed to look at our reflections. And now I was hearing of something similar in the Jewish religion.

"Chris, you should let Jack know about this. He can find the Israeli cops that are working on Gabe's homicide."

"I think my telephone card's at the hotel." I sighed.

"Go up to our room and use our phone," Hal said.

"Take the kids?" Mel asked hesitantly.

Hal gave her a big grin. "Of course I'll take the kids. Come on, guys. Let's see if we can find a *Herald Tribune* somewhere in this hotel."

"Daddy, would you buy me the hat we saw in the store with the newspapers?" Sari said.

Hal laughed and led them away.

"He's good," Mel said as we walked toward the elevators. I agreed.

It was a pretty long conversation, because Jack wanted to get everything right. "This is a good one," he said finally, after he'd checked names and addresses and times and events. "We've got police departments five thousand miles apart working on the same case."

"I'm not sure we'll ever get everything coordinated," I said.

"We've really got to find out what, if anything, was taken or disturbed in Marnie's house."

157

"Mel and I are going to call her, Jack. Mel says she'll be home accepting visitors, so we shouldn't have too much trouble finding her."

"Ask if she has a home safe. And know what? She might just call the office where Gabe worked and find out if anyone broke in there, especially if they have a safe."

"I'll ask."

"Tell her to call the local police and ask them to look for prints on the safe, if she has one. There shouldn't be any except his and hers. She mustn't touch it till they've been there. And I'll let Joshua know. I doubt whether the police in the States have been in touch with the cops here."

"Interestingly complicated."

"See you later."

I wrote down the things he was interested in and looked at my watch. It was too early on the East Coast to call. We went downstairs and Mel rescued her husband and took over their children. Hal had made arrangements to spend some time with a couple of his cousins and he took off. I rather wished I had my own son with me so he could have the pleasure of being with friends for a few hours, but that wasn't possible. So I decided to hook up with Mel and her kids till this afternoon.

What we did was take a taxi to the Old City to visit the Citadel. The taxi turned out to be a problem. Mel gave our destination and we had gone about a block when I realized the driver hadn't turned on the meter. I leaned forward and asked politely that he do it.

"It's too late," he said. "I have to charge you five shekels from where I picked you up."

"Five shekels!" Mel said with feeling. "It's a block or two. Just turn it on."

"I make you a special price," he said.

"I don't want a special price," she countered. "I want the meter."

He said something neither of us could understand. Then he repeated that he would give us a special price. We looked at each other. There seemed to be nothing we could do. When we reached the Citadel, we argued — or rather, Mel argued — that his price was too much and he dropped it two shekels. I felt very uncomfortable about the whole thing. I wasn't used to haggling over prices and I was used to having taxi drivers turn on their meters the minute you sat down in the cab. I was sure Mel and I had overpaid, but I couldn't determine how much.

"Let's forget about it," I said when we

were walking toward the ticket window at the Citadel.

"Hal warned me." She sounded angry.

"Officer Davidson warned me, too. I see what he meant."

But the tour around the Citadel was wonderful and made up for the trouble we had getting there. An American man who had lived in Jerusalem for twenty years was our guide, and he took us through the ins and outs and ups and downs of the ruins, stopping frequently to give us a piece of history. The kids enjoyed the beginning and got bored as we went along, but they hung in till the very end. We stopped and bought postcards, and I got a beautiful book full of pictures of the ruins. If Jack couldn't enjoy them with me, at least he would be able to look at what he'd missed.

Near the Jaffa Gate, where we had entered the Old City, we found some taxis waiting for customers.

"I'll handle this," Mel said sternly as we got inside one of them with a big, hefty driver encouraging us to enter. Inside, she said, "Please turn on the meter."

"What you want the meter for?" he said, pulling away toward the gate.

"Because that's the way it's supposed to be."

"I give you a good price."

"Turn on the meter!" There was no mistaking Mel's fury.

"So who are you," the driver asked with annoyance, "a colonel in the Israeli army?"

"A general," she retorted. "Turn on the meter."

He turned it on.

The trip back to the hotel ended up costing considerably less than the "good price" we had paid without the meter in the other direction. The driver grumbled as he drove; traffic was against him and the lights weren't working right. Mel and I stifled giggles.

"Glad I teach third graders," Mel said when we had both gotten out of the taxi. "It prepares you for the tough times in life."

I laughed. "You were wonderful, Mel. I couldn't have done it myself."

I went up to her room and we placed the call to Marnie. Someone who wasn't Marnie apparently answered and called her to the telephone. Mel talked to her for a few minutes, asking about the funeral and a few other things. Then Mel brought up the break-in, or whatever it was. "My friend Chris is here," she said finally. "Do you have the energy to talk to her? . . . OK then. We'll talk again. Here's Chris."

161

I took the phone and said a few polite words to Marnie. Then I asked about the security system.

"Chris, I was so depressed and confused, it didn't even register that something was wrong. I went inside, pushed the buttons, and hung up my coat. It took a while before I realized something was wrong."

"What exactly was wrong?" I asked.

"The whole system wasn't working. I mean you could lock and unlock the door and the system didn't do anything. I suddenly saw that there weren't any lights flashing on the panel. I called the company and they said they'd noticed something was wrong but hadn't had a chance to send anyone out here. But they did. He looked it over and said someone with a lot of knowledge about that system had disengaged it."

"I suppose he didn't know how long ago that had happened."

"Actually, he thought it was sometime on the Sunday Gabe was kidnapped." She sighed. "I told Gabe I didn't like them. We should have gone with another company." She spoke as though what had happened was a mere annoyance.

"Marnie, do you keep a safe in the house?"

"Yes. No one could find it without a thorough search."

"Have you checked to see if it's been disturbed?"

There was silence.

"Marnie?"

"You think someone came in to steal something?"

"I'd like you to do a couple of things if you can. First, without touching the safe, see if the dial is on the last digit you turn to to open it."

"OK. I'm on my way to it now. Just a minute."

"Remember, don't touch it."

She made a sound as though she was pushing something, perhaps moving a piece of furniture out of the way. "The safe's locked," she said. "I just pulled it with a napkin and it didn't yield. And it's not set on the last number in the combination. It's a different number."

So the last person to open the safe had rotated the wheel after closing it. "OK. Leave it alone for now."

"What now?"

I could tell she was walking away from it. I could hear the sound of voices somewhere, people visiting to comfort the widow. "Have you notified the police?" I asked.

"No. Why should I?"

"Because your security system was tampered with. Somebody may have gotten into your house. Ask the police to come out and check the safe for prints."

"This is unbelievable."

"And call your husband's office and see if they've had a break-in recently."

"You're serious."

"Very. If we're going to find out who's behind this tragedy, we've got to look into everything."

"Yes. All right."

"After the police leave, you should open the safe and see if anything is missing."

"Chris, do you honestly believe this has something to do with Gabe's murder?"

"It's a coincidence, and it's good to be skeptical of coincidences."

"I suppose so. When is this going to end?"

I felt sorry for her. To have all these burdens at the same time must be shattering. "Who has the combination?"

"No one except Gabe and me."

"What do you have in there?"

"Jewelry, papers."

"Expensive jewelry?"

"Yes. Very."

"What kind of papers?"

"I really don't know. Our wills, I suppose. Life insurance. Maybe the deed to the house."

"Let us know what happens. Please check with Gabe's office. And call the police as soon as possible."

Mel and I hung around, hoping Marnie would call back. We weren't disappointed. About an hour later Mel's phone rang. She handed it to me right away.

"I called the police as you suggested, Chris," Marnie said. "They dusted the safe, put tape all over the door, then pulled it off and opened it. Then they took my fingerprints to compare with whatever they find. I assume someone in Israel has Gabe's."

"Probably," I said, hoping the medical examiner had done a thorough job.

"I won't get an answer on that till tomorrow at the earliest. But after they left, I opened the safe and looked inside. Chris, if anyone got in there, they must have just looked. I swear, nothing's been touched; nothing's been moved."

"Do you keep a list of what's in there?"

"I do. The insurance company said I should. I didn't have a chance to check everything, but I'm sure it's all accounted for. I would have opened the safe myself if you hadn't gotten to me first. I need all those papers when I see the lawyer."

"I'm sure you do. Did you reach anyone at Gabe's office?"

"Yes. I called them before the police came. There hasn't been any break-in. They seemed surprised that I asked."

I noticed Mel was writing something on a piece of hotel notepaper. When she finished, she passed it to me. I looked at the note and asked, "Does anyone live in the house besides you, Marnie? Like a housekeeper or gardener or caretaker?"

"Yes, I have a housekeeper. But I told her to take as much time off as she wanted while we were gone. Honestly, I didn't expect trouble."

"So it's possible no one was in the house for a number of days."

"Very possible."

"Marnie, ask the housekeeper when she was away. Try to get exact days and times. This may help the police and the alarm company determine what happened and when. And I'll call you or Mel or somebody when I know what's going on."

I hung up and shook my head.

"You think Gabe was killed so someone could steal Marnie's jewelry?" Mel asked.

"It's possible. The men who kidnapped him may have beaten him for the safe combination. It was a great time to rob their house. No one was home."

"I'm sure they must have lights that go on

166

and off and people who are paid to look out for the house."

"They can't do it every minute of the day," I said. "If you're an expert on security systems, you probably know how to disable them. Then all you need is a key."

Mel looked at me. "Which they could have stolen from Gabe after they kidnapped him. And flown back to the States with. My God, this could really have happened."

"You take the key off his key ring," I said, working out the details. "You get on a plane — you've made the reservation a long time in advance — and fly to New York. It doesn't really matter whether Gabe's alive or dead. Marnie isn't thinking about protecting their house five thousand miles away. Everyone's so concerned about what's happened right here. There was something in that safe, Mel. I bet they got the combination out of poor Gabe. What could they have been after?" I said it more to myself than to Mel, but she said, "Just what I'm thinking."

"Well, we had a nice day. I'm really glad we got to see the Citadel."

"So what's next?"

"I have to find out more about Gabe. Somewhere in his life or his marriages or his work there's something that should set off an alarm. When it rings, I'll hear it."

15

I drove back to the hotel thinking about the possibility of looking into people's pasts from a distance of five thousand miles. I wished desperately that Joseph were here, but it would be futile to imagine she could make the trip. She had a convent to run and a college to oversee, not to mention a budget that was scarcely enough to take care of the nuns and the buildings.

I had about half an hour or a little more before I had to pick up Jack, and I decided to look into the lovely shop across from the hotel within the compound. It was run by a tall dark-haired Arab who greeted me graciously as I entered. He sat behind his counter, a pair of tiny white ceramic cups on a small matching tray before him. The cups were empty but stained with recent coffee. I supposed he had a friend, perhaps in a nearby store, who came and joined him for coffee and talk.

The shop, which also had a downstairs filled with rugs, was almost overflowing with interesting Middle Eastern goods, most of them handmade. There were things made of brass, glass, leather, wood, and combinations of all four. I could have bought a little table inset with mother-of-pearl or necklaces with appealing beads or a rug to put beside our bed at home in Oakwood.

The owner remained unobtrusive, which pleased me. I don't react well to hard sells, and I really enjoyed looking at all the things he had accumulated. What attracted my attention the most was a mirror with mother-of-pearl designs inset in the wood frame. Telling myself I was absolutely not buying anything, I asked the owner what the price was.

He came over, looked at it, and said, "That's a Druse mirror made of lemonwood."

"Really?" I ran my fingers on the smooth wood.

"It's sixty-five dollars."

"Thank you," I said, rather glad that it was more than I was willing to pay. "When my husband is free, I'll ask him to come in and look around. I think he'll enjoy it."

The owner smiled and said he would be happy to have my husband visit the store.

I went back to the hotel to read the paper for a while before picking up Jack.

★ ★ ★

"You think Marnie could be lying to you?" Jack asked as he drove back to the hotel to freshen up before dinner.

"Why would she lie if something was stolen? Wouldn't she want it back?"

"Sometimes the reasons why people lie are elusive. Maybe she had stolen goods in the safe and she can't report them stolen because she'd end up being arrested for theft."

"Come on, Jack. Marnie didn't steal anything. She's a wealthy woman."

"Just giving you a for instance."

"I just can't believe the security company didn't take it seriously when the system went off."

"Let me tell you about security companies," Jack said, and I knew I would now get a lesson. "When a client's system goes offline temporarily and they pick it up on their screen, it's a very low-level priority of theirs. It could be weather. Maybe a rat gnawed a wire." I felt my skin crawl. "All the security company has to go on is the screen indication, which could say 'line trouble.' That could be a downed telephone line but no real alarm. They give the local cops a call when they get around to it. Eventually, a cop'll drive out to the house, rattle the doors, give the place a walk-around, see that

170

nothing's wrong, and he'll get back in his car and continue his rounds. The only way he's going to react is if he finds evidence of a break-in or an unlocked door."

"So what you're telling me is that neither the cops nor the security company is very interested in following up on something like this."

"Remember, no one called in that there was a problem. The cops may or may not know that the owner of the house is away."

"They might not," I agreed. "Marnie has a housekeeper that lives in the house, but Marnie told her to take as much time off as she wanted. The Grosses didn't really know when someone would be in the house and when they wouldn't."

"So the Grosses probably didn't bother mentioning that they would be five thousand miles away for a week or so."

"Did you get a list of Gabe's personal effects?" I asked. "I'm interested in the house key."

"In fact, I did. I'm not connected to the case so I'm on nobody's list, but I got hold of an inventory today. It's in my briefcase, but don't bother opening it. The key ring is there and what is probably his house key is there, too. He probably left all his unnecessary keys home, maybe in that safe of his.

171

There are a couple of car keys on the ring and what looks to be a key to a house. If Marnie were here, we could have her identify it."

"Then how did they do it, Jack? I figured someone flew back to the States with Gabe's key and they waited to dump his body till after they got into the house."

"They didn't have to fly anywhere." Jack turned into the street where the hotel was and then into the compound. I loved the greenery. "Is that a space?"

"Looks like it."

"Glad I'm not driving a big American car."

"We could never afford the gas here." I had blanched when this little car with its economical stick shift had had its small tank filled to the tune of twenty-four dollars.

"Glad to see you're not getting corrupted."

He got out and we went upstairs, Jack pulling off his shirt as we got in the room. "Maybe I'll start dressing down like everyone else in this country."

I looked at him in shock.

He laughed. "Just kidding. But it's a nice idea and no one seems to care around here."

"You said they didn't have to fly anywhere," I prompted him. "The key."

"The key. Right." He sat down and pulled his shoes off. "Here's how these guys do it. You take a key off the ring, lay it down on a piece of foil, and fold the foil carefully over the irregular side of the key, making a foil duplicate. Then you Xerox the foil and fax it back to the States.

"If they had a locksmith involved, it would be very easy. The locksmith looks at the key, notes the brand and the 'cuts,' the little hills and valleys, and simply uses a blank to cut a duplicate. If this 'dupe' was a little off, it could be dressed up with a Swiss file as they tried it in the door. Most locksmiths are honest guys, but hey, money talks."

"And you put the key back on the ring, put it in the victim's pocket, and it's there when the body is found."

"Exactly. Meanwhile, your fax arrives at its destination and is used to make the new key. Back in the old days, keys were duplicated from wax impressions. No more. The new key works in the lock and no one ever took the key anywhere."

"That's fantastic."

"Technology," Jack said offhandedly. "The good guys develop it and the bad guys use it to their advantage."

"So they didn't even have to take Gabe's key to a fax machine and rush to get it back.

They could dump his body any time they wanted and the key was in his pocket, just as it was when he was kidnapped."

"You got it."

"Wow," I said.

"But none of this tells us whether anyone made a key and got into the house and, if they did, whether they opened, or tried to open, the safe."

"Because if they used a key they made the way you described, we can't prove it, and if Marnie doesn't find anything missing, how do we know it happened?"

"And it's just possible that the security system went down because of a fluke like bad weather or telephone line trouble."

But I was more convinced than ever that it wasn't a fluke, and I suspected Jack was, too, and that someone had gotten into Gabe Gross's house as he lay dying five thousand miles away.

"Why did they beat him, Jack?"

"Good question. I'd guess to find something out. The other possibility is that someone really hated him and wanted him to suffer."

"They wanted the combination," I said. "And they kept him alive until they got word from the States that someone had gotten into the safe."

"Which means they got into the safe — if that's what they did — the day after Gabe was kidnapped, or maybe even that Sunday night."

And then they finished him off and dumped his body, I thought. "A very well coordinated operation," I said.

"So how come Marnie says nothing's missing?"

He ducked into the bathroom, leaving me to ponder the question. And ponder I did. One of the things I've learned in the years I've been looking into homicides is that you can't automatically exempt a person from suspicion because he's such a nice guy or, in this case, such a nice woman. How would any of us know what Marnie found or didn't find in that safe? Even assuming there was a list of the contents of the safe, she could easily rewrite it before she showed it to anyone. If she was hiding a theft, how could I figure out what was missing without, for example, talking to her insurance company? And perhaps she hadn't bothered to insure things that were in the safe, considering them immune from theft.

Obviously, I needed to find out more about Marnie, but I didn't think that her husband's family would be privy to the kinds of details that would be useful to me.

I started to change my clothes and saw a folder on top of Jack's attaché case. It was marked "Inventory" and I opened it to find a sheet of paper with a list. They were Gabe's possessions on the last day of his life.

All the clothes he was wearing were listed. There was also a gold watch and a gold wedding band, both engraved. A linen handkerchief, monogrammed. A leather folding case containing an American passport, American money and Israeli money, photographs of unnamed people, a medical insurance card, a driver's license, several credit cards, and a membership card in an organization I had never heard of.

I could think of several things that an American man would be likely to have in his wallet that were not listed. One of them would be the registration to his car. Another might be a library card. Possibly a number of membership cards to professional organizations and the kinds of clubs Jack and I don't belong to. What that meant was that Gabe had weeded out the things he needed on the trip and left the rest of the contents of his wallet at home. Where had he left them? Probably in his safe, since he had one. And probably he had never recorded those items on the inventory.

In his pocket were coins from Israel and the U.S. And then there was the key ring. The keys were enumerated in the inventory. One was assumed to be a house key, two were car keys, another a key to a suitcase or small lockbox. Two keys were unidentified. I had to be right that he had taken only keys he would need on his trip and on his return. I walked over to the dresser and looked at the ring of keys Jack had taken with him. He had left nothing home and he had so many, I teased that they weighed him down. Gabe, of course, was a more experienced traveler than we were and knew better than to carry what was unnecessary.

I picked up the phone and called Mel, catching her in her room before they left for dinner. "Mel," I said, "were any of Marnie's relatives invited to the Bar Mitzvah?"

"No. We were mostly Gabe's relatives and a couple of his old friends. Children weren't counted, by the way. There were actually more than the forty I told you about because several of us brought our kids, and Gabe reserved a room for them, but he didn't invite his in-laws."

"Any reason?"

"I think he felt this was a family thing. Why?"

"I really need to know more about

Marnie, and I guess I'd learn more from one of her relatives than from one of Gabe's."

"You're probably right. She kind of walked into the family as his wife. They didn't have a big splashy wedding, just parents, brothers, and sisters. She didn't dress up in a fancy white dress."

"Who are her closest relatives?"

"Let's see. She has a sister who's younger and a brother who's older."

"Parents?"

"Both living, I think."

"She doesn't have any kids, by any chance, does she?"

"Not that she's made public."

"I see."

"I did hear she had a miscarriage, so they may have wanted to have one child together."

"Do you know anything about her brother and sister?"

"Oh, gosh. I really don't. I'm not sure I've ever even met them."

"OK. If you think of anyone who's here that might know about her, let me know."

"I'll tell you, it's getting tougher and tougher. Everybody's leaving. Maybe you'll just have to wait till we all get back."

"That's what I'm thinking. The answers don't seem to be here. Whoever orchestrated this plan just wanted to make sure Gabe and Marnie would be far from home and couldn't get back quickly. I don't know how we'll ever figure out what was in that safe when they left and what, if anything, was stolen."

"I'm sure Marnie knows."

"I'm not so sure, Mel. Maybe Gabe had something he didn't tell her about. If it's gone, she won't be aware. And maybe she knows and doesn't want to tell."

"That's an interesting thought."

"I'll talk to you tomorrow. I've got to dress for dinner."

At dinner I related the story of Mel and the taxi drivers to my rapt family. My mother-in-law, who is no shrinking violet, was surprised and rather delighted by the tale.

"She sounds like a spunky person, your friend."

"She is. I really admired her for the way she stood up for our rights. I don't think I'd be able to do it myself."

"Well, now I see why the cabdrivers are always trying to make deals with us," my father-in-law said. "I thought they were being nice to strangers."

We all laughed.

When Jack and I got back to the hotel, he said, "Have you reached the point yet where you want to talk to Sister Joseph?"

"I don't have enough, Jack. About all I know is that someone made a very intricate plan to kidnap and kill Gabe Gross. I don't even know if they originally planned to kill him or just get that key from him and the combination to the safe."

"You may never know that."

"True. I don't know what I could tell Joseph that would give her enough to come up with something. I think the answers are in the States, somewhere in Gabe's background, as you suggested, or in Marnie's life."

"So you've given up on his relatives?"

"I only interviewed a few and I got nothing from them. Including Hal and Mel. Mel says most of them have left for home by now. What am I missing?"

I must have sounded rather forlorn, because Jack gave me a grin and patted my back. "You're missing the key. We all are."

"What are the Israeli police looking into?"

"The usual things — drugs, black-market deals, covert shipment of military equipment. His name doesn't come up anywhere."

"Has anyone tried to get a copy of his will?" I asked.

"They've asked. I'll check tomorrow and see if it's come yet."

"Maybe that'll shed some light," I said.

16

While I was driving Jack to the police station the next morning, I asked him if he knew where Gabe's body had been found.

"It was on a street," he said, "in an Arab district. Someone went outside and found it and called the police."

"Is there a house address?"

"You want to go there." He didn't sound happy.

"I really should. After we leave, anything I've missed I've missed forever."

"Look, I'll find where the place is, but I don't want you going there by yourself. Just a precaution."

"Maybe I can get Hal to come with me."

"I hope he doesn't sue me when he sees where you're taking him."

"I'll protect him. After all, he's my friend's husband."

Jack got out of the car and gave me a kiss. I drove back to the hotel and waited for his call. I really wanted to do something and there didn't seem much to do at this end, unless the location of the body led me somewhere productive. About fifteen minutes after I got back to the room, Jack called with the address. He cautioned me firmly and I promised not to be stupid. The truth was, I was too scared to be stupid. There's something about being in a foreign country that makes everything worthy of suspicion.

"What did the police learn from the canvass?" I asked.

"Nada. This is a group that doesn't like the police."

"Good," I said brightly. "Maybe they'll like a woman who isn't police."

Jack had said the area was called Silwan and it was located below the Dung Gate, to which I made an appropriate comment. But that's what that gate to the Old City is called. The neighborhood had once been part of Jordan, and the people living and working there were Arabs. It was definitely accessible by car.

I found the street on the map, then picked up the phone and called Mel's number.

No one answered and I decided, considering the time, that they were probably at breakfast. If I hurried, I could get to them before they left the hotel.

I was lucky. When I got to the house phone, they had just come back to their

183

room. I talked to Mel, then to Hal, then to Mel again. I could tell Mel was dying to come with me and Hal didn't want her to. We finally decided to drive over in two cars, with Mel sitting next to me to navigate and Hal and the kids following. When we were done, they could take off and I could go my own way.

I sat down in the lobby to wait and suddenly the little round man of yesterday morning appeared.

"Good morning," he said pleasantly. "You are still in Jerusalem."

"Yes, we're staying several more days."

"But you are not at the hotel you told me you were staying at."

My heartbeat signaled panic. He had checked up on me. "I beg your pardon?"

"I went to the American Colony to talk to you. You are not registered."

"Mr. Kaplan — What is this about? Why did you go to my hotel?"

"I thought perhaps we could continue our conversation. There is no one named Bennett registered at the hotel."

"I'm registered under my husband's name," I said, feeling a little better. "I'm sorry; I didn't think you were going to look for me."

"I have things to tell you."

Something about him began to annoy me, but I didn't want to give up a source. "I would like to hear your information," I said, hoping he had something I didn't already know.

He didn't look very happy. "If you really want to know how Gabriel Gross died, you should set aside some time so we can talk."

I looked beyond where he was sitting and saw Sari and Noah charge out of the row of elevators. "I'm sorry. My friends have just come down. We have somewhere important to go." I stood and picked up my bag. "Call me at my hotel."

"Miss Bennett." He sounded insistent or perhaps irritated. "Your husband's name?"

"Brooks," I said. "John Brooks. I have to run."

Mel studied the map for a few minutes when we got to my car. "It'll take us a while, but so what? What do you expect to find there?"

"I have no idea. It just seems to me I ought to cover every base before we go back home."

"You're right. Who was that little man you were talking to?"

"I wish I knew. He claims to know things about Gabe and Gabe's father, but he won't

185

talk except under his conditions. I can't set aside a lot of time. Which way do I turn from here?" We were at the curb, leaving the hotel parking lot. In my rearview mirror I could see Hal clearly.

"Left. If you can."

"I'll do my best."

The buildings on the street where Gabe's body had been found were old and two stories high. They were, of course, made of the same Jerusalem stone as the rest of the city, but they had a distinctly shabby look to them. Laundry dried on lines between and behind buildings. Dark-haired children played noisily on the street. I turned into an alley and stopped the car, leaving enough room behind me for Hal to park his. We got out.

"No wonder Jack didn't want you to come alone," Hal said, joining us. His children were sitting in the backseat of their car, peering out the windows. "Where did they find the body?"

"In one of those alleys, Jack said. Not on the street we drove on."

"What do you want to do?"

What I wanted to do was leave and forget about this. I assumed the police had canvassed the area as thoroughly as they did in the States when a crime occurred. "I want to find out exactly where the body was left and who found it. I guess that means I have to knock on doors."

"You think they'll speak English here?"

"I'm crossing my fingers."

"Let's go."

Mel got into the car with her children, and Hal and I walked up the stone steps to the nearest dwelling and knocked on the door. A woman dressed all in black opened the door and listened to me introduce myself. Then she responded in what I was pretty sure was Hebrew. I looked at Hal, but he just shrugged. The woman smiled, showing two missing teeth, and closed the door.

"Don't say anything," I said to Hal. "Maybe we'll have better luck next door."

"You're a plucky lady," he said. "I hope that doesn't count as having said something."

I laughed. The next door yielded only a slightly better conversation. The woman who answered knew a few words of English but assured me she knew nothing about a body. I wasn't even sure she knew what the word meant.

Hal and I continued from house to house, smelling odd food odors as doors opened, but accomplishing nothing. One old man said in quite good English that he had spoken to the police and there was nothing more to say. I asked him exactly where the body had been, and he told me to ask the police.

When he closed the door, Hal said quietly in my ear, "I don't know if you've noticed, but there's a guy watching us. Don't turn. I'm keeping my eye on him."

We started walking. "Where is he?"

"Right now behind us. He was standing outside one of these houses and then he started to follow us."

"Maybe I should approach him."

"I get the feeling he wants to approach us, but he's scared."

"Stay here, Hal." I turned away from him and started back, seeing a painfully thin young man about twenty feet from me. He stopped walking as I began to move toward him.

Suddenly he smiled. As I approached, he said, "You are an English lady?"

"I'm American," I said.

"You want to talk?"

"I want to know if you saw the body here last week, the dead American man."

"Yes, yes. I see the dead man."

"Will you tell me about it?" I spoke very carefully, not too fast, keeping my voice modulated. He seemed so frail, I was afraid of scaring him away.

"My mother, she tell you."

"Does your mother speak English?"

"No. I speak English. I am study in England for six months."

"That's wonderful," I said. "You speak very well."

"Yes?"

"Yes, you do."

When he smiled, I could see how crooked his teeth were, how they were filled with black spots.

"You come this way."

I looked back at Hal, not sure whether he should join us. He was practically at my heels.

"Where're you going?" he asked.

"No, no," the young man said. "No man. Just American lady talk to my mother."

"You going with him?" Hal said.

"He says his mother saw the body. Can you wait outside his apartment?"

"Chris, I don't know. You may not be safe."

"No police," the thin fellow said. "American lady only."

"This man's not the police. He's my friend. He will wait outside for me. Is that all right?"

"Outside is all right."

We walked past a couple of buildings and

then up some stairs. My guide was wearing a stained white shirt and black pants with sandals. His hair was collar-length and raggedly cut. He reached into a pocket and pulled out a key that opened the door. Hal hung back. I waved as I followed the young man inside.

The room into which we walked was crowded with furniture, and the tile floor was covered with a worn Oriental rug in dark reds and blacks. There were no lights on and it was pretty dark, but I could make out a plump woman, her head covered with a shawl, sitting on a sofa. I didn't like the smell in the room, but I thought I could tolerate it long enough to learn something.

"This my mother." He said something in another language to the woman, who smiled and nodded several times. She then pointed to a chair and I sat down.

"My mother see the American man dead. You know this American?"

"Yes," I said, deciding to stretch a truth that would be too difficult to explain.

"You ask my mother now?"

"Did she see the man?"

He asked her a short question and she responded at length, arms moving. "He have a cover, like a bed." He seemed to be searching for a word.

"A blanket?"

He smiled. "A blanket. Yes. My mother look inside blanket. All blood on shirt. Eyes open. My mother very —" He acted out fear.

"Afraid," I said.

"Afraid. My mother afraid."

"Did she call the police?"

"No, no. No police."

"But the police came."

"Yes."

"Did she talk to them?"

"No police. My mother, no police."

"I understand. Then someone else called the police."

"Maybe someone."

"Do you know who called them?"

He shrugged.

These people clearly weren't giving anything away. I wasn't sure why he had been so anxious for me to talk to his mother when she seemed to have little to say except that she had lifted the blanket and seen the body. "Did your mother see the people who put the dead man in the street?"

He asked her. She answered briefly.

"She see two men."

I had my copy of the drawing made from Marnie's description. I took it out of my bag and handed it to the woman. She nodded vigorously and spoke to her son.

"This is the man. This the man with the American dead."

I took the sketch back. "Did your mother see the truck?"

He looked as though he had not understood, then smiled and spoke to her again. "She see lorry. Truck. Yes. She see it."

"Did she see them take the American man out of the truck?"

"No," he said, translating. "She see the truck after."

"Did she see anything that would help me find the truck? Did she see a number on it?"

When he spoke to her, she reached under the layers of fabric she was wearing and extracted a piece of paper. She handed it to him. He looked at it and said something to her. Then he said to me, "This for you. From truck."

I took it from him and looked at it. She had copied what looked like a license plate number in soft pencil that was now slightly smudged. I felt the excitement of having actually learned something meaningful that the police might not know. If all the people in this group of buildings were as reticent to speak to the police, and to me as well, I could imagine the police had learned very little. Perhaps the only reason they had been called when the body was found was to get rid of it.

"Is this the license plate number?" I asked.

"Yes, number of truck. My mother see number and write it down."

"This is really very helpful," I said. "Is there anything else?"

The mother shook her head and he said that was all. "No police," he said. "You understand?"

"Yes, I do." I stood and offered him my hand, but he didn't take it. I thanked him, then thanked his mother, who smiled and nodded, as though she had understood me. Then I went outside to where Hal was worriedly pacing.

"Get anything?" he asked.

"I think so. The woman wrote down what looks like the license plate number."

"No kidding. That's pretty damn good."

"They're terrified of the police. They didn't offer their names and I didn't ask. I'm going to find a phone and call Jack. Maybe he can run the plate and I can find out who that fake ambulance belongs to."

"Get anything?" Mel came toward us as we neared the cars.

"She's good," Hal said. "She may break this case yet."

Mel grinned. "I told you."

We stood there for a few minutes deciding whether to split up. I wanted to go back to the hotel and call Jack from there so I would be sure to have enough time to talk to him. These phone cards had a nasty habit of cutting you off unexpectedly just as you were about to say something important.

"You know what?" Mel said. "There's a great pottery place right near your hotel. Hal's cousin told me about it last night. Why don't we drive over with you, you make your phone call, and we'll all go over there together?"

"You're taking the kids to a pottery place?" Hal said.

"My kids are very well behaved." Mel seemed hurt by his implied suggestion. "So are yours."

He smiled. "Then let's do it."

17

"You got what?" my unbelieving husband said in my ear.

"The plate number. This woman copied it down. I'm not even sure she's literate, but she had a pencil, with a thick, smudgy point, and a piece of paper and she wrote it down."

"Can you make it out?"

I read it off to him as best I could. "Can you find someone to run it?"

He laughed. "You're telling me you want to stay one giant step ahead of the cops."

"That's what I'm telling you. Can you do it?"

"I'll give it my best shot. Where are you?"

I told him, and told him what the plan was with the Grosses. "If you get anything, leave a message here at the hotel. I'll check back after we destroy the pottery shop and have lunch."

"Keep my name out of the destruction, OK?"

"You bet."

When I got off, I started to think about

the little man in the hotel lobby this morning. Perhaps I had been too abrupt. If he came back to talk to me, we might be out to dinner. I decided to call and leave a message if he didn't answer. I wouldn't mind talking to him with Jack around; in fact, I'd prefer it.

I called Mel's hotel and asked for Simon Kaplan's room. The operator came back and said, "I'm sorry. No one by that name is registered."

"He's checked out?" I asked in surprise.

"One moment, I'll transfer you."

A man answered this time and I repeated my request. He assured me Mr. Kaplan was not registered. I asked when he had checked out.

"I have no record that he was registered here in the last week."

I was stunned. "Thank you," I said. Now what? I thought. Either he isn't who he said he was or he's registered under another name. Or maybe . . . I reached for the telephone book to look up the hotel the Bar Mitzvah party had been held in and realized, once again, that the book was printed in Hebrew. I called the operator and she got the number and connected me.

No, I was told, there was no Simon Kaplan registered. I asked her to check the date of the kidnapping. No, she said tiredly when she returned, he had not been registered on that day, either.

Something very strange was going on, but I couldn't pursue it at the moment. The four Grosses were downstairs waiting for me. I picked up my bag and went to find them.

"Looks like they have a great outdoor restaurant," Hal said when I got off the elevator.

"They do. Maybe we can have lunch here when we get finished looking at pottery."

He laughed. "Looking? Are you kidding?"

We rounded up Mel and the kids, who were peeking into the shop across from the hotel entrance, and drove a couple of blocks to the street where the potter was. Just before we reached the American consulate, Hal spotted what was probably the only open space at the curb and somehow managed to back into it, meriting applause from the two adult women in the car. We got out and walked down the block to the Palestinian Potter and went inside.

It was a large place divided by a corridor the length of the business. On the right side were windows beyond which were mostly women hand-painting pieces of pottery. We stopped and watched, the children absolutely transfixed.

"I could do that," Sari said almost in a whisper.

"Maybe we'll sign you up for a ceramics class when we get back," Mel said.

"What's sramics?"

"It's making things out of clay. There are classes for kids at the temple."

"Ohh," Sari said dreamily, and I smiled. She was an artistic child, making pictures that seemed well beyond her years, and I thought Mel's suggestion was a really good one.

Across the corridor was a door to the shop. Hal cautioned the younger Grosses to keep their hands at their sides and walk slowly, and we went in. It was a very long store with tables and shelves filled with beautiful things. Some of them were similar to the pieces we had seen at the shop in the Old City; some were very different and much larger.

Hal was as taken with the pottery as Mel and I were. He agreed they should get several small bowls and divided dishes that they could serve chips and dips in. I thought hummus was a better idea and said so.

"Ah, Chris, you may never go home after this experience." Hal handed me one of the divided dishes and I agreed we could use one, too. I liked the dark blue with the fish pattern and found one on a table.

But what Mel and I really fell in love with were the two large plates that hung high on the wall. They had religious and symbolic drawings on them and typical Armenian border designs. Mel said she had to have one, and a very willing shop owner got a ladder and took them down. Eventually, I decided to splurge and take whichever one Mel left behind, as I liked them equally.

"We can trade off," she said breezily. "Six months here, six months there. I just love them."

Hal persuaded me to use my credit card, as I would get the best rate that way, and I set aside my inborn prejudice against charging. When we left, Mel and I each had one huge package wrapped in bubble wrap and a smaller one besides, and we were thrilled.

We had lunch in the garden, the adults all ordering the platter of various salads that was served on a dish not too different from what Mel and I had both just bought. There were hummus and orzo and several other delectable items.

"I think I'm in love with hummus," Mel said, wiping the last of it up with a piece of pita bread.

"And you pronounce it so well," I said. "I just can't get that back-of-the-throat sound."

"You will. Just keep eating it."

We parted and I went upstairs to find a message from Jack that said to call him back.

"Here's the deal," he said. "Joshua's not around, so I feel sort of OK giving you the info. But the minute I find him, I tell him."

"Sure."

"This plate is on a van that has not been reported missing, so I'm a little reluctant to have you chase it down. You could be dealing with the guys that kidnapped Gabe."

"I'll watch myself," I promised.

"Where have I heard that before? Anyway, it's a store that sells touristy things downtown, not too far from Ben Yehuda Street." That was the name of the famous walking street. He dictated the address and the name of the store owner, Moshe Karpen.

"I'm on my way," I said.

"I've been told parking's almost impossible there, Chris. Why don't you get a taxi?"

"OK. I'll practice what I learned from Mel."

"Yeah, sure. Take care of yourself."

I went downstairs and had the doorman get me a taxi. I was a little nervous getting in, remembering the last time and Mel's vendetta against the driver. But to my happy surprise, the driver turned the meter on as soon as I closed the door and told him where I wanted to go. He let me out at the intersection of Ben Yehuda Street, which sloped downhill, and King George Street. I was so pleased, I gave the driver an extra shekel for his honesty, but I didn't say why.

I got my bearings and found the shop. It was one of those stores with a million objects for sale, everything from postcards to olive wood camels and key rings with crosses or stars of David — an equal opportunity vendor.

Outside there were a couple of people looking at postcards and inside there was one woman looking at all the things for sale, several already in her hand. I went to the middle-aged woman behind the counter.

"Yes?" she said, observing that I was holding nothing to buy and probably assuming I needed directions.

"Mrs. Karpen?" I asked.

"Yes?"

"I want to ask you about your truck, your van."

Her face darkened. "What about it?"

"Can you tell me where it is?"

"What kind of a question is that?"

"Do you know where it is?"

"Of course I know. It's at my house."

"It is?"

"What is this about?" She spoke good

English but with a slight accent that I could not identify. It was obvious my questions had disturbed her.

"I think your van may have been used in a crime."

Her look turned to one of fear. She called toward the back of the store, "Moshe?" and added some words in Hebrew. An older man came out, a skullcap on his head. They exchanged a few sentences in Hebrew. Then he took his place behind the counter.

"Come with me," the woman said, moving toward the back of the shop.

I followed her into a small crowded room with a desk and an open door to a bathroom.

"What are you saying?" she said.

"You have a van with this license plate number." I showed her the slip of paper the woman from the crime scene had given me.

Mrs. Karpen moaned.

"That's your van?"

She nodded.

"Where is it, Mrs. Karpen?"

"I don't know. I don't know."

"It's not at your house?"

She shook her head.

"Where do you think it is?" I didn't want to suggest that it was stolen. If she believed it was, let her come up with that herself.

"Maybe someone took it."

"Who?"

"This is terrible. You said a crime. What kind of crime?"

"A very serious one. The police are searching for the van. They'll probably be here later."

"Oh, my God." It was almost a whimper.

"You know where the van is, don't you?"

"I don't know. I swear I don't know. I haven't seen it for weeks."

"Why didn't you report it stolen to the police?"

"I couldn't."

"Do you know who has it?"

She nodded.

"You should tell me, Mrs. Karpen."

"Why you? Who are you?"

"I'm looking into a crime. I have to turn my information over to the police. It's better if you admit it now than if they find out later."

"I know." She closed her eyes and took a breath.

Neither of us had sat down in the crowded little room. There was a chair behind the desk and a second chair, a molded plastic one that took up little space, but we had both stood. Now she sank into the chair behind the desk, put her head in her hands, and said nothing. I waited, hoping she would tell me what I needed to know.

"It's my nephew," she said, looking up. "He's a good boy, but he gets into trouble sometimes. He took it once before, a couple of years ago, but he brought it back. I couldn't report it to the police; he's my sister's only child." She seemed near tears.

"And you're sure he has the van?"

"What else could it be? It's not such a great van anyone on the street would want it."

"Have you talked to your nephew?"

"I talked to my sister. She said he doesn't have it."

I wasn't all that surprised that a mother would respond that way. "Will you give me their names and addresses?"

"Oh, my God. My sister will kill me."

I said nothing. She opened the top drawer of the desk and took out a piece of paper, then grabbed a pencil and wrote on the paper from right to left.

"In English, please," I said.

"Oh, of course." She wrote underneath the Hebrew and I marveled at how she could switch languages and alphabets in a second. What a feat, I thought. She handed me the paper. "Will you go now?"

I tucked the paper in my bag. "What color is your van?"

"Light brown. Tan."

"Does it have writing on it?"

"Like the name of the store? No. It's just a van. It has a good motor and we take good care of it."

"When did you notice it was missing?"

She sighed. "What's today? Tuesday? Before last week. Maybe two weeks ago, maybe on Wednesday or Thursday of that week."

Which gave them time to paint the van with several coats of white so it would look like an ambulance. "Thank you, Mrs. Karpen."

"You're gonna talk to my sister?"

"I'm going to try."

"Don't tell her I told you. Please."

My next taxi gave me a little trouble. He took off from the curb and I asked him to turn on the meter. He started to say he would make me a special price, but I told him I didn't want a special price, I wanted the meter. Growling, he flicked it on.

This trip took me to Bethlehem Road. It was a street of houses and stores, groceries and dress shops. The driver let me off in front of a building that looked the same as the ones on either side, and I went inside and rang the doorbell marked "Schloss" in English letters and in Hebrew as well.

Someone inside called that she was coming and then the door opened. The woman looked remarkably like the one I had just left in the center of town, but this one was slightly plumper and wore her hair pulled back, more as though she wanted it out of the way than as a fashion statement.

"You're the woman about the van."

"I —" I was startled.

"My sister called me. What do you want to know?" She made no move to invite me in.

"The van is missing."

"That's what my sister said."

"There's a chance your son may have borrowed it."

"Borrowed? Is that what she said to you?" She gave me a grim smile.

"The police are looking for the van."

"Well, I hope they find it. Is there anything else?"

"A crime was committed, Mrs. Schloss. The van may have been involved in that crime."

"Let the police prove it then. Is there anything else?"

I had started to say something when I heard a male voice call from somewhere in the apartment, "Hey, Mom?"

"Is your son home?" I asked.

"It's none of your business."

A young man in his twenties appeared behind her. He was dressed in jeans and a tight black shirt that showed bare, muscular arms. He was eating something and had a bottle of beer in his hand.

"Mr. Schloss," I said, pursuing my opportunity, "I'd like to talk to you about the Karpens' van."

"My aunt's van?"

"Yes. Where is it?"

"Get out of here," his mother ordered as he spoke above her words.

"Don't ask me. I haven't seen it for a long time," he said.

"How long?"

"Coupla weeks anyway."

"Who has it?"

"Shut up!" his mother shouted. "You, whoever you are, go away." She tried to shut the door, but her son kept it open.

"Couldn't tell ya." He sounded American and I wondered if they were new arrivals in Israel or he had gone to school in the States.

"Did you take it, Mr. Schloss?"

He put the beer bottle down on a table, probably leaving a ring his mother would kill him for, and wiped his mouth with the back of his hand. "Can we talk outside?"

"What are you talking to her about?" his

mother almost screamed. "You don't have the van; there's nothing to talk about."

"I'm going out for a while, Mom. I'll be back soon."

Mrs. Schloss tried to bar his way, but he passed her without pushing and walked outside. Behind us the door slammed and the bolt turned. I wondered if he had a key with him, but I guessed it didn't matter. His mother would let him in, no matter what.

18

We went to a little place a block away that had tables and chairs and also did a take-out business. I ordered a juice and he ordered coffee. On the walk over, he had told me his name was David.

"What do you know about this van?" he asked when we were sipping our respective drinks.

"I think it may have been involved in a crime."

He muttered an obscenity that was barely audible. "What kind of crime?"

"A very serious one, David. If you had anything to do with it —"

"Do you think I'd be asking you questions if I knew what you were talking about?"

I ignored his hostility. I was pretty sure he was nervous about what I knew. "All I know is that the van was seen near a crime scene."

"So maybe my aunt committed a crime."

"The van disappeared several days before the crime was committed."

"So that makes it my fault."

"I didn't say that." The van certainly wasn't parked on the stretch of Bethlehem Road that we had walked. "But if you have the van or if you know where it is, you should come forward."

"I don't have it."

"Did you take it?" I asked, sounding rather tentative.

"I didn't take it. I —"

I waited. I was sure now that he knew where it was.

"I can't even say I know who has it — or had it — because they didn't . . . uh . . . I just don't know who they are or where they are."

"Did you give the van to someone?"

He closed his eyes and let his head drop. Then he shook himself, as though trying to wake up, and drank some more coffee. A man about his age came in, saw David, and walked by, talking to him in Hebrew and slapping his hand against David's. David said something and the other man walked away.

"They said they needed a van. I owed them money, OK? I told them where they could find a van, but they had to get it back. They said they only needed it for a couple of days and then it would be dropped off where they found it. I knew my aunt wouldn't report it if it got back in a few days."

"And they forgave your debt."

"You could say that."

"When did they take the van?"

"I don't know the exact day. Maybe two weeks ago."

I took the police sketch out of my bag. "Is this one of the men who took the van?"

He looked at it and muttered his obscenity again. "Where did you get this?"

"Some people saw him committing the crime. A police artist drew this."

"You're not gonna tell me what the crime was."

"It was a serious crime."

"You said that before."

"What is this man's name?" I asked although he had already said he didn't know who the men were.

"Believe me, if I knew, I would tell you. They never brought the damn van back. My aunt's been calling my mother, my mother keeps saying I don't have it, which is true, and I'm in deep — I'm in trouble. And I didn't do anything."

I didn't correct him. "Do you know who this man works for?"

"He works for himself as far as I know."

"What did he say he needed the van for?"

"He didn't say exactly. I got the feeling he was picking up some things for resale."

I smiled at the circumlocution. "Resale."

"Yeah. At a profit."

"Maybe he used it for that, but he used it for other things, too."

"How do you know about all this?"

"It's complicated, but I know relatives of the victim of the crime."

"Somebody got hurt?" He shoved his empty cup and saucer across the tiny round table.

"Badly hurt, yes."

"They ran somebody down with the van?"

"I can't discuss it any more than what I've said. I think you ought to try to locate these men so the police can find them."

"The police are coming to get me?"

"I wouldn't be surprised."

"How could this happen?"

I didn't think he seriously wanted the question answered. I paid for both our drinks, went out to Bethlehem Road, and hailed a taxi back to the hotel.

It had been the most successful day of my investigation. I called Jack and gave him the names and addresses. He said Joshua had been in touch with him earlier and was probably at the Karpens' store.

"And by the way, I have a copy of that will for you to look at. It was faxed to us today or yesterday, not a great copy, but you can make it out. I haven't looked at it yet. I'm trying to get work done so we can have a good weekend."

"I'll see you later."

I really wanted to talk to Sister Joseph. I could not think of a motive for the murder of Gabriel Gross. His wife said nothing was missing from the safe. If she was telling the truth, then the whole incident of the compromising of the security system was probably a coincidence and we would never know if a copy was made of Gabe's house key. If she was lying, she might well be involved somehow in her husband's death. But why?

I called my in-laws and found them at their hotel. I drove over and spent some time with Eddie and his grandparents before he decided to ditch me permanently and take up residence with these wonderful people he was traveling with. It turned out to be a very pleasant hour and a half for all of us. I did most of the listening, amazed at my in-laws' skill at scheduling their time.

"You should see what Eddie's been eating, Chris," my mother-in-law said at one point. "He's absolutely fearless when it comes to new foods."

"Well, that's a blessing. He obviously has his father's palate, not mine. Although I must say, the food has been wonderful."

"I like hummus the best," Eddie said, making an almost perfect sound at the start of the word.

"My goodness, you even pronounce it right," I said with surprise.

"Well, you know what they say about learning foreign languages when you're young," my mother-in-law said.

"I guess they're right."

"Can you make it when we get home?" Eddie asked.

"I'm sure we can. Mel will show me. We'll have to find a place that sells pita bread."

"It's in Prince's," my observant son said. "I saw it there."

"Then I guess we're all set." I leaned over and gave him a kiss. It was absolutely fine with me if he turned out to have his father's powers of observation as well as his fine palate.

When I left, I drove directly to the police station and waited at the curb for Jack. I was a few minutes early, so I turned off the motor and watched people walking in and out of the building. About five minutes after I arrived, Joshua Davidson came out, looked around, saw me, waved, and walked over. I leaned over to unlock the passenger side so he could sit down.

"Mrs. Brooks, I didn't know you were a secret investigator."

"It's not much of a secret where we live. I've been written up in the local newspaper. I hope you're not angry that I went to the Karpens and their nephew."

"I might be, but I was so happy you got that license plate number, I forgave you. We talked to about a hundred people in those houses last week. No one had any information for us."

"They're terrified of the police. The man who took me to see his mother, the woman who had written down the number, said they wouldn't talk to the police. I suspect they've got something to hide or think they do."

"No matter. That was a remarkable discovery. How did you find him?"

"He found me. He must have seen me going from door to door asking questions — and getting no answers, by the way — so he followed me. I don't think he saw anything himself, but he knew his mother had."

"Well, thank you."

"Have you found the van?"

"No, but we're working on it." Standard police talk for "we haven't accomplished anything." "I think your husband has a copy of Gabriel Gross's will with him. Maybe you can find something in it we missed."

I smiled. "You're very kind. I will certainly read it tonight."

"And on your last night, my wife and I would like to make an Israeli dinner for you, if that's all right with you."

"That's wonderful. This has been the most interesting and unusual trip of my life."

"When you come back, I promise we won't have a homicide to interrupt your visit."

Jack walked over to the car at that moment and the two men exchanged a few words while I got out and switched to the passenger seat. Then we were off.

After dinner I studied the will. There was a lot of it that I didn't understand, and although Jack said his knowledge of estate law was kind of thin, as he had forgotten most of it after he passed the bar, he was able to explain what the trusts were that Gabe had set up for members of his family. There was also a good deal about the ownership of the company, but none of it seemed suspicious. Gabe's children, whom I believe he still loved dearly in spite of the estrangement, had the right to many of his shares in the business. Or they could sell their interest to people who were now working for Gabe, the price to be determined by a formula. It looked pretty well thought out to me, and I wondered what the son and daughter would decide to do.

Marnie was very well provided for, as was any child who might have been born after the writing of the will or she might be carrying at the time of Gabe's death. His ex-wife also got a lump sum bequest, but nothing like the amount he left for his current wife. Not surprising. I wondered if Debby knew she was mentioned in his will.

There seemed to be none of those tricky devices where one person got more if Gabe died at a certain time or in a certain way. The will was straightforward. He just wanted the people he cared about most to inherit his wealth and he wanted the business to succeed. He also named a number of charities that would benefit. I had heard of a couple and never heard of the rest, but I think many organizations that do good works are unknown to the general population.

"Anything set off an alarm?" Jack asked as I laid the pages on the desk.

"I wish I could say yes. It all seems in

keeping with what I've heard about him. His family came first, his business was very important to him, and he was philanthropic. I didn't find any strange name that could be an old girlfriend or blackmailer mentioned. It looks like a dead end."

"I know you're itching to talk to Sister Joseph."

"I am, but it's very expensive to call. When we do this kind of thing in her office, we take a long time."

"You know we can afford it. They're paying most of our expenses here."

I shrugged. Sometimes the thought of spending a lot of money makes me feel a little ill. All of this goes back, I'm sure, to the days of my living at St. Stephen's, when everything I earned was turned over to the convent and the convent gave me spending money when I left the grounds. Spending money in those days was generally fifty cents unless I was taking a trip. For most of the years that I lived there, the last of those years as a nun, I used my nun's dowry to fill the tank of my car with gas, and my aunt was generous when I visited her, which was once a month. It has proven to be difficult for me to shake the feeling of having very little and the discomfort of spending a lot all at once.

"Why don't you call her tomorrow,

Chris?" Jack said. "Figure out a good time and call from here. Try to put the call on your credit card so it doesn't show up on our hotel bill."

"I'll think about it."

"Boy, you're a tough one."

"You know we're having dinner with the Grosses tomorrow night. It's their last night."

"Already?"

"They're leaving Thursday."

"And Friday we're taking off for our last weekend."

"Why don't we huddle over a map and forget Gabe Gross for a while?"

"What are you doing today?" It was Mel's voice on the phone. I had just come back from dropping Jack at work.

"No plans at the moment, except for our dinner tonight. I've got a map on my lap."

"Open to suggestions?"

I laughed. "Mel, your suggestions always cost me money."

"No, they don't. Sometimes they get you a good lunch."

"True. OK. I'm open."

"There's a wonderful shop we haven't seen yet."

I laughed again. "Doesn't sound like

lunch to me. There must be fifty wonderful shops I haven't seen."

"There are. And I'll leave you a list. But this is one I haven't been to and my aunt said I had to go. I've got the driving directions. Interested?"

I almost said no. Then I thought, Come on, Kix. You may never come this way again. "Sure. But I have to be back this afternoon to call Sister Joseph. I want to get her while it's morning there."

"I'll run out of money before then. And I have to pack."

"I'll pick you up at nine-thirty."

19

Until we attempted to find this last shop, I had gotten the feeling that I really knew the city. But this was an unexpected challenge.

"If you drive by the King David Hotel on your right, you make a right turn just after it."

"I think it's going to be on our left, Mel."

"Mm. Right. Then you take a left before you get to it."

"But I don't know I've gotten to it till I've gotten to it."

"Fear not. I will guide you. Can you believe there's a street here called Lincoln?"

"I can believe anything."

"When we see Lincoln on our right, we turn left."

"Where is it we're going?"

"Hutzot Hayotzer."

I said nothing. The words were just too much for me.

"Are you with me?" Mel asked.

"I am with you all the way." I inched the car into the street. "What's my first turn?"

It was pleasing to recognize streets and buildings as we drove. I actually sensed we were approaching the King David Hotel when Mel said, "It's coming, our turn. Stay left."

There wasn't more than one lane of functioning traffic in each direction, but I made sure I was near the center of the street.

"Lincoln," Mel said triumphantly. "Turn left."

I made the turn after waiting for a long line of cars to cross the intersection. Behind me, a horn sounded. I had learned to take it in stride. They did the same in New York, I told myself. "What now?" I asked as I completed the turn.

"My aunt said it's a curvy street, all downhill. Just follow it."

Her aunt had not exaggerated. The street went around and down for quite a stretch. "Are we near the Old City?" I asked.

"Yes. Very near."

"OK," I said finally. "We've bottomed out. What now?"

"Uh, let's see. Go left."

I turned.

"See the parking on the right? Pick your spot. We've arrived."

We had indeed. The parking lot was behind a long row of buildings. We got out and walked around the buildings to a street that was more of an intermittent staircase with shops on either side.

"It's on the left," Mel said. "Just a little ways up."

And then we were there. We stopped to look in the window that ran across the front of the shop. Everything in it was beautiful and intriguing and, I was sure, far too expensive for my pocketbook.

"It's Roman glass," Mel said. "About two thousand years old."

"The colors are fantastic."

"My aunt said the Romans tossed their garbage out the window, it got buried, and in the earth the glass, which was clear to begin with, picked up minerals from the earth and turned all these incredible colors."

"I'm not buying anything," I said defensively.

"Who are you trying to convince?" Mel gave me the grin.

"I'll just watch you have a good time."

We went inside. I scanned the shelves while Mel introduced herself as her aunt's niece. The owner, a pleasant-looking man with dark hair starting to recede and a warm smile, recalled exactly what the aunt had bought and welcomed us cordially. While Mel was busy with earrings and pendants, I admired small animals made of Roman glass and silver sitting on open shelves, marveling at the work that had gone into them. I saw chains with unique links, a bracelet that I realized was a piece of the Jerusalem skyline. There were some pieces in gold, too, and they were breathtaking.

"I'm getting something for Sari, Chris. Help me out."

I walked over to the counter, looking at the earrings and pendants lying on black velvet. "This is lovely," I said. "The blues and greens are wonderful."

"Do you think it's too big?"

"Mm."

"How about this one?"

"This one" was yellows, browns, and greens. And it was smaller. "Stay with the blues," I said. "She'll grow up."

"Done."

"What a lovely cross," I said, looking at one in the case.

"Are you Christian?" the owner asked.

"I'm Catholic."

He took the cross out and I held it. He put it on a chain and I fastened it around my neck. "Lovely," I said again, taking it off and laying it down carefully.

"My friend is not in a buying mood," Mel explained.

The owner smiled and put the cross back in the case.

"It's really nice, Chris."

"I know."

"Sari's going to love this. And I'm going to love the earrings and now I have to get something for my aunt. She commissioned me."

"What a nice task."

"You bet."

I wandered around the small shop once again. "I'll wait for you outside," I said, leaving her to her pleasure.

I went up the steps to the street at the top and realized the wall of the Old City was just across the street. I turned and went back down, looking at the shop windows on the other side of the walking street. As I reached the shop, Mel came out.

"What did you get your aunt?" I asked.

"Earrings. Great store, huh?"

"The best we've seen."

"That's a beautiful cross."

"It gives me a reason to come back."

It was Mel's last day. We found our way back to Nachalat Shiva, where we had our first lunch last week, and had our last one together at the same place. Mel was nostalgic, sad at leaving, happy she had come, and reflective about Gabe.

"I have to say," she said when we were sitting at one of the little round tables waiting for our hummus salad and Cokes, "I don't think anyone will ever find out who killed him."

"We've made progress, Mel. The young man I talked to yesterday, David Schloss, who arranged for those men to take the van, I think he may know more about who they are than he's letting on. The police may be able to get something out of him."

"I hope so. With all of us leaving the country, there won't be anyone here to put pressure on them. Gabe was a good man. Whoever did this should pay a price."

"Don't give up."

We made a quick tour of the shops, but just to look. Then I dropped Mel at her hotel and went back to the American Colony and called Joseph.

She was as surprised to hear my voice as I was happy to hear hers. We spent only a minute or two on small talk. Then I told her about the kidnapping and murder of Gabriel Gross.

"Chris, what a terrible thing to happen. On such an important and happy trip."

"With all his closest friends and relatives around," I added. "It's quite mysterious."

"And that's the purpose of your call."

"I just didn't want to wait till we got home to talk to you. In case there's something that strikes you as important that I can still look into while we're here."

"Well, I've just reached over for my stack of clean paper and I have a couple of sharpened pencils nearby. Let's get started."

As I usually did, I had my notebook open to the page where I had begun jotting down facts and impressions. I went through them in chronological order, finishing with my productive day yesterday, the interviews where the body had been found, the scrap of paper with the plate number of the fake ambulance, and the subsequent trip to the Karpens' store near King George Street and Ben Yehuda Street, followed by the taxi ride to Bethlehem Road.

"Oh," I said after I had told her about the talk I had with David Schloss that included his admissions about the "borrowed" van, "I read Gabe's will last night."

"And?"

"And there isn't anything you wouldn't expect to find in the disposition of a rich man's wealth. It all looks quite in order."

"No unidentified names getting substantial sums? No, that's a foolish question. You've thought of that. So what do we have? A man enjoying one of the happiest occasions of his life, surrounded by the people he loves the most, and he's whisked away when he apparently falls ill and no one finds him till he's dead."

"Exactly."

"And at home, five thousand miles away, a possible illegal entry of his house."

"Possible, yes."

"But nothing missing either from the house or from the safe."

"Marnie didn't mention the house, but I expect we would have heard from her if she'd found something missing. She said nothing was gone from the safe."

"And you believe her?"

"I don't know. I have no reason not to. And she seems genuinely distraught at the events."

"Understandably. Chris, the young man who borrowed or allowed the van to be taken, what's your appraisal of him? Do you think he was involved in this?"

"I don't. I can't imagine he would have spoken to me if he'd had a hand in this. He could very easily have ducked out when he saw me at his mother's door. But he seemed genuinely curious about what was going on."

"And the police have still not found the van or the men who were in it."

"Not unless something happened in the last few hours."

"If the house was actually entered, then we've had important events on this side of the ocean. I would imagine all this was orchestrated from the United States by someone with connections to Israel."

"I agree."

"Another thing: If Mrs. Gross had had a hand in this, why wouldn't she just have given someone the security code and the key, as well as the combination to her safe? Then there would have been no need to hurt or eventually murder her husband."

"True."

"Which would indicate that she knew nothing about this murder. Unless, of course, she was planning to leave her husband because there was someone she wanted to take up with — and have her husband's money to boot."

"The family seems to think she's a good and loving wife."

"It wouldn't be the first time a family misjudged a situation like this. However, it's something I can't really say anything about. It's the break-in that's so intriguing, Chris. Why break in if you don't take anything?"

"The question we've all been asking ourselves for several days."

"There is, of course, another possibility."

"Oh?" I said, feeling eager for her next comment.

"It's always possible that they didn't break into the safe to remove anything. They may have put something in it."

"Mm," I said, my head starting to work. "Any ideas?"

"Not offhand, but it's something we should both think about. What would someone put into a safe?"

"And why would Marnie not mention that she had found it?"

"Maybe because she isn't aware of it. Someone could have substituted a fake jewel for a real one. I'm sure I've read books where that was done."

"Then I should ask Marnie to have her jewelry looked at by an expert."

"It might be a good idea. What else did they keep in that safe?"

"Important papers. Insurance policies, things like that."

"And they're all there, too."

"So she said."

"Well, this must be costing you a fortune, Chris, and I know you're not a spendthrift. Let's both think about this. If anything else comes up, there's a less expensive way of reaching me. Believe it or not, Sister Dolores's niece gave her a laptop computer for her birthday. It has e-mail on it and she'll be glad to print out your message and deliver it to me."

"Dolores?" I said. "What a wonderful gift." Dolores was one of Eddie's favorite nuns. She's a great cookie baker and always has a bag of goodies for him when we visit together.

"From a wonderful woman. Anyway, it's good to have someone here who knows something about the Internet, whatever that is." She gave me Dolores's address and I wrote it on the pad next to the telephone.

"We circled the Sea of Galilee last weekend, Joseph," I said.

"Chris, we will have to spend an afternoon together when you return. Those words have given me goose bumps."

"And me, too, while we were there. And I was taken on a guided tour through the Old City."

"And went to the Church of the Holy Sepulchre."

"Yes."

"Before I am done in by envy, we'd better say good-bye."

"You'll make this trip yourself one day; I promise."

"That will certainly be the day. Kiss your son for me, please. And a big hug to your husband."

"I will do that."

20

I called Mel and got Marnie's phone number. I wanted to tell her to take her jewelry to a qualified person and have him look at it. The phone rang several times and was picked up by the housekeeper, who was reluctant to bother Mrs. Gross. I explained where I was calling from and Marnie picked up a moment later.

"This is Chris," I said.

"In Jerusalem?"

"Yes. I have to ask you something. The jewelry you keep in your safe, is it diamonds and other precious stones?"

"Some of it. I also have gold chains and some expensive watches."

I sketched out what Joseph had said.

"You think someone replaced real stones with paste?"

"It's possible. We have to check out every possibility. Someone killed your husband and we don't know why."

"But I've never lent my jewelry to anyone. No one could substitute a fake if they hadn't seen or photographed the real thing."

"Maybe they photographed it when you were out."

"You mean a friend of ours did this?" She sounded incredulous.

"They may not have intended to kill Gabe, just get into the safe and exchange the jewels."

"It's preposterous."

Her reaction didn't surprise me. Had someone suggested that one of our friends had done something similar, my reaction would have been exactly the same. "Will you ask someone to look at your jewels, Marnie?"

Something like a moan traveled the wire. "Yes. You're right, Chris. I have to look at everyone and everything. I'll let you know when I've done it."

I decided to go downstairs and look at the shop across the way once again. As I got off the elevator, I saw a familiar face. I walked over. "Mr. Kaplan," I said.

"Ah, here she is." He turned away from the desk and smiled at me. I didn't smile back. "I hoped I would find you, Mrs. Brooks."

"Mr. Kaplan, I don't know who you are, but you aren't who you said you were."

"Of course I am. What seems to be the problem?"

"You aren't in the hotel you said you were in. I called."

"Yes, you're right. I checked out."

"You were never there." I looked him straight in the eye.

"You're mistaken, my dear. Why don't we have a cup of coffee and talk?"

I thought that was fairly safe, so we went to the garden restaurant. We ordered coffee and he asked them to bring some small cakes. I had the feeling I was being buttered up.

"I'm sorry the hotel told you something false," he said when the ordering was done.

"I also called the other hotel, the one where Gabriel Gross was kidnapped from. You weren't a guest there, either." I heard myself sound rather unfriendly, but I was getting tired of being lied to. I thought he was spying on me, trying to determine how much I knew. Whom he represented I could not imagine. I don't think of criminals as roly-poly men in their seventies, but perhaps that is just a vestige of age discrimination.

"Ah, Mrs. Brooks. You are indeed a detective. I assure you, I have not lied to you. I was a friend of Gabe's father, I knew Gabe as well. I saw the ambulance, just as I described it to you."

"Who were the men driving it?" I asked.

"I told you, I have no idea. I saw the driver at the wheel —"

"Yes, I remember your story. What else do you have to tell me?"

The coffee was served. He dropped a cube of sugar into his cup and stirred it with the small spoon, not looking at me. "I am a businessman," he said finally, taking a sip of his coffee. "Please help yourself to some cakes. They're very delicious."

I took one, waiting for something of substance to come from this man.

"A mostly retired businessman nowadays, although I don't like to think of myself that way. I knew Gabe; I knew his father. I did business with both of them. I am as anxious as you to find out who kidnapped and murdered Gabe."

"Then why don't you take what you know to the police? I'm a tourist here in Jerusalem. I'm only interested in the Gross case because I know a cousin of Gabriel. If you know something, the right thing to do is give it to the police."

"I rather think not." He helped himself to a chocolate cake and ate a small forkful. "Have you made any progress finding the killer?"

I was really feeling very frustrated at this

point. "Mr. Kaplan, you said you wanted to help me, but in fact, you're pumping me for information. I don't know who you are or what your real name is."

He reached inside his jacket and pulled out a U.S. passport and passed it to me across the table. I opened it and looked first at the picture. It was definitely of the man opposite me. Then I checked the name. Simon J. Kaplan. I handed it back to him.

"You see, I am who I say I am. If I shaded the truth a little when I told you where I was staying, I apologize."

"You didn't shade the truth; you lied to me."

"Well, let that be. In business, I was a diamond merchant. I was a member of the Diamond Dealers Club in Manhattan."

"What could diamonds have to do with Gabe's work?"

"Sometimes people convert assets into stones. Such business makes the assets both liquid and easily portable."

"Are you telling me that Gabe did?"

"I am telling you I did business with him."

"Why are we talking? Is there something you want to tell me? Because I don't have a lot of time." I looked at my watch pointedly and realized that what I had just said was no exaggeration.

"Have they found the ambulance Gabe was taken away in?" he asked rather casually.

"I doubt it."

"Do you know where it is?"

"Do you?"

He smiled. "I have an idea. I believe it was stolen and I think it has been returned, or will be soon."

"Mr. Kaplan, how can you possibly know that?"

"I have sources. I believe Gabriel Gross was in possession of stolen diamonds when he was kidnapped."

I stared at him. "How do you know that?"

"I don't know it for certain. I believe it to be true. Not all his business was kosher, as we say."

I knew the expression. "Where did these diamonds come from?" I asked.

"The source is a little unclear."

"Are you saying he was killed for those diamonds?"

"I'm saying he was kidnapped for them. Why he was killed is a mystery to me."

"Perhaps he didn't have them and they killed him trying to find out where the diamonds were."

"That would be a logical conclusion."

"Did he acquire the diamonds from you?"

He smiled. "No, my dear. He did not."

"Were you expecting to acquire them from him?"

"As I told you, I am largely retired. And I don't deal in stolen merchandise."

"I don't know why you're telling me these things," I said.

"I'm trying to help you."

I couldn't see how. The suggestions he was making struck me as wild. I hadn't known Gabe Gross, but I was very reluctant to think of him as a criminal. I looked at my watch again. This conversation was making me very uncomfortable. "I really have to go," I said. "Thank you for the coffee. It's been very pleasant." I got up and left the table before he had a chance to ask for the check.

I stood in the lobby for a few moments, trying to decide what to do. Then I went back up to my room. I didn't want to see this man again. I didn't know if he was telling me facts or obfuscations. I didn't understand all of what he was saying. And I couldn't, for the life of me, figure out what his purpose was in telling me these things.

I sat in our room for a while, looking over the *Herald Tribune*. I felt quite annoyed. I had wanted to visit the shop, but instead I had wasted half an hour listening to vague accusations that led nowhere. Finally, I changed for the evening so Jack could have sole use of the bathroom when he got back. Then I went to pick him up.

When he was in the car, I told him about Simon Kaplan. "He's an annoyance," I said.

"Sounds like it. If he shows up while I'm there, I'll get rid of him for good. OK with you?"

"Fine."

"I don't like the whole thing. What's this talk of diamonds? Didn't Marnie say nothing had been taken from the safe?"

"Yes. And she has an inventory. I'm sure she would have told me if something like diamonds was missing. It's not the sort of thing you overlook."

"I don't get this guy."

"I don't, either."

"Well, let's forget about the whole thing and have a good meal. Hal's got a reservation at a French restaurant that he says is supposed to be great."

"French," I said in surprise. "What's a French restaurant doing in Jerusalem?"

"You think Israelis only eat hummus?"

"I would if I lived here."

"Give up all those tuna sandwiches?"

I thought about it. "Maybe I'm ready."

"Wow. Never thought I'd hear that from my wife."

★ ★ ★

Our dinner was incredible. The men fought over the check at the end and Hal won. It must have cost a fortune, but the meal was excellent, really French. We said our good-byes at our cars. The Grosses were leaving the next day, and Mel promised to look in on Eddie regularly till Jack and I got back. As we were staying till the middle of the following week, Jack's parents had agreed to stay with Eddie in our house so he could go to school. Two weeks was long enough.

During dinner I asked Hal if he knew anything about Simon Kaplan, and he didn't. But he thought that a connection between Gabe and diamonds was a stretch. The closest he came to diamonds was giving them to his wife.

When we left, Jack drove up to the university, which is at a high elevation, and we got out and walked around. The air smelled fresh and the sky was clear. The stars were different from the New York area, but eventually I was able to find some familiar constellations. I have always wondered what the sky looked like in Bethlehem on that special night, and although I am not likely to get there, this was pretty close.

Students walked by, looking for all the

world like the students I teach in New York State. They giggled the same way, walked as couples the same way. And stopped to kiss the same way. It was nice to know there were still some absolutes in the world besides the Ten Commandments.

Jack and I were sitting on a low concrete wall. "I'm going to look up this Kaplan guy in my database tomorrow," Jack said. "See if he turns up."

"Well, he showed me a passport."

"He could have another one in another pocket."

"I didn't think of that."

"He could register in the hotel under one name and give out another."

"Which would make him unfindable. How would he get another passport?"

"He could have picked one up in France or England after the war. If he was a refugee, they'd probably give him papers without a lot of hassle. People didn't have documents when they were let out of concentration camps. Or if he worked for any government agency, he would have access to people who could get things done in irregular channels. Europe's records were a mess by the end of World War Two."

"Ah. Yes, he does have a very slight accent. He's probably not American by birth."

"So he may not be in the database with the name he gave you."

"It gets more and more complicated," I said.

"They always do, till you get to the end."

It was the same old story.

21

I felt a little sad the next morning. Today I was completely on my own. There were several places I wanted to visit, but I would have to check the map carefully and write myself clear notes that I could glance at as I drove, since my super navigator was winging her way home.

I dropped Jack off and went back to the room to get myself set for my day. My first stop would be Yad Vashem, the Holocaust memorial site.

It was a beautiful spot. Inside in the dim light of the cavelike atmosphere, I felt the magnitude of all the deaths, all the suffering. As I had many other times, I wondered how people could treat other people so harshly.

Outside, the sun blinded me for a moment and tears formed in my eyes. I brushed them away and began to walk along the Street of the Righteous Gentiles. Here were the names of some people who had helped, who managed to save lives. I read every name.

It was an awesome experience. I had weighed whether or not to visit this place, but I was glad I had. I would remember it in a special way.

I had lunch and did a little more sightseeing before I returned to the hotel. Jack and I had decided to spend our weekend in the western part of the country, and I wanted to check routes on the map and mark the places we hoped to visit. I sat at the desk and figured out how we would drive. Like last Friday, I would pick Jack up and we would take off.

As I was making notes, the phone rang. When I picked it up, I recognized Marnie Gross's voice.

"Chris? Is this a bad time to call?"

"No, not at all. Is something up?"

"I want to talk to you. When are you coming home?"

"Next Wednesday."

"That's almost a week away." She sounded very unhappy.

I explained about Jack taking extra week-end days and how he had to make it up at the end.

"I don't know," she said.

"Don't know what?"

"I have to talk to someone. I trust you, Chris. You seem to know what you're doing and you're not family."

I smiled at that. There was something positive about not being family. "Maybe you should talk to the police about whatever it is."

"I can't."

I waited, but she said nothing more. "What is it, Marnie? You called me all this distance away. It must be important."

"It is." She said something that sounded more like a moan than a word. "I found something in the safe that's not on the inventory."

"I see." I could feel anticipation building, remembering what Joseph had said. "You have the inventory?" I asked.

"I found it, yes. Everything on it is in the safe, but there's something else in there, too. Gabe must have — I don't know. Maybe he put something in at the last minute and didn't write it down."

"Will you tell me what it is?"

"It's — I don't know, Chris. It's very upsetting. He never said a word to me about it. I think maybe he was planning to give me a present."

"A present."

"It's a small bag. I didn't see it at first. Then, when I went over the contents of the safe with the inventory in my hand, I spotted it. It has some diamonds in it, loose diamonds, each one wrapped in something that looks like pale blue parchment. That's what I wanted to tell you."

"Diamonds," I said, trying to keep from sounding as surprised as I felt.

"Five, I think. A good size. I have a beautiful diamond engagement ring. These are all larger than that."

"You're right," I said. "He must have been planning to surprise you."

"Why aren't they on the inventory then?"

"I don't know."

"I'm not doing anything with them, Chris. They're in my safe, so they belong to me. Everything in that safe belongs to me. It's just, as I said, I was unsettled when I found them."

"I can understand why. Marnie, I have a question to ask you."

"Sure."

"Do you know a man named Simon Kaplan? Or did Gabe know him or mention him?"

"It doesn't ring a bell."

"He's in his seventies, I think, rimless glasses, kind of roly-poly, a pleasant-looking man."

"No, I don't think so. Why?"

"He approached me in the hotel you were

staying in. He claims to have done business with Gabe and his father."

"Really?" She sounded surprised.

"That's what he said. He told me a few things that seemed to be helpful, but in the end, I don't think they were. He makes me uneasy. I just wondered if the name or description rang a bell."

"I can call Gabe's secretary and ask."

"That would be a good idea. Let me know, OK?"

"I will. I'm writing down what you said. Chris, will you call me as soon as you get home? I want to see you in person and talk to you about what I found."

"I'll call you when we get back."

"Thank you, Chris. Thank you very much. I feel better now that I've told you."

I wondered if I did.

I called Jack and told him Sister Joseph might have been on the right track, that Marnie had found something in the safe.

"You gonna tell me what or leave me hanging?"

"Jack, this has to be between you and me."

"What does that mean?"

"You can't tell the police what Marnie told me."

"I foresee a problem."

"That's why I'm saying this. If you feel obliged to pass along what I know, I won't tell you."

"Why?"

"She told me in confidence. It took her a while before she said it. She's very nervous about this. I can't be responsible for having the police show up at her house with a warrant. I'm not saying anything else till you give me a promise."

"You'd better keep it to yourself. If you tell me something material, I have to run with it. You know that."

"OK. I'm getting things together for our trip tomorrow. I'll see you this evening."

"You bet."

I felt very awkward. These things had come up before, but not quite this way. This wasn't an informant giving me information that would lead to a killer; this was an innocent person — at least, I believed she was innocent — telling me something that might involve her husband or herself in suspicious activities. The fact that Marnie had told me, the fact that she had been so reluctant, made it seem that she knew nothing at all about the diamonds she had found in the safe. Had I not met Simon Kaplan, I would have assumed the same thing she had, that Gabe had bought some diamonds to make a gift for her. But I had met Simon Kaplan and I could not figure out how all these pieces fit together. It simply couldn't be a coincidence that the little man had mentioned diamonds twenty-four hours before Marnie admitted to finding the stones in her safe.

22

I picked Jack up at the usual time and got into the passenger seat as he neared the car. He slid inside and gave me a quick kiss, then started the motor and took off.

"Looks like your digging on the fake ambulance was a good lead."

"They find it?"

"It was returned to the owner. Karpen, I think, is the name."

"Just like that?"

"Yup. Joshua went over and talked to them himself. Then he hauled in the nephew and gave him a hard time."

"Oh, dear," I said.

"He's OK. But he gave up the names. Or one of them."

"The ambulance attendants?"

"If you want to call them that."

"Then we're close," I said.

"Well, not that close. Either they really don't know who they were working for or they're good at what they do. They said it was an American, no name, everything in cash; you know the drill."

"What were they supposed to do?"

"Just what they did. Kidnap Gabe Gross, make a copy of his house key, find out the combination to the safe. Also the code to the security system, but they had a set of priorities. The code was last on the list, and by the time they got the safe combination out of him he was dead."

"How horrible."

"But they claim someone else killed him, if you want to believe it. They figured they could get by the security system, but they couldn't get into the safe without the combination. It was all very carefully worked out."

"And what were they supposed to do when they opened the safe?"

"These guys claim they have no idea, and I believe them. That was all on the U.S. side of things, out of their hands. But they swear they had nothing to do with beating Gabe to death and I don't believe that for a minute."

"If they didn't do it, who did?" I asked.

"They're playing dumb. Some mysterious guy showed up, took over. It's all crap. They did it. Joshua agrees."

I found myself agreeing, too. There were enough people involved in this business already, two in Jerusalem, one or two in the

States; it was hard to believe there was also an expert in beating someone to death. "So we've got two killers in custody and we still don't know who ordered the kidnapping and killing."

"Right. If they're telling the truth. They may not be. Remember the Schloss guy told you he didn't know who these two were and, of course, he did. It just took a little probing to get it out of him." Jack made the turn across traffic into the street where the hotel was. I always held my breath as he did this.

"Well, I'm glad those two are in custody, but I have the feeling the police and I are no closer to figuring out who ordered this."

"But you've made a lot of progress. The answer may be in the States."

"Marnie wants to see me when I get back."

"So she's got more to tell you, huh?"

I smiled. "That's what she says."

"I have a feeling she may be the key."

"Well, I'll know next week. I don't think she's going to tell me over the phone, and I'm not bothering her about this. I just want to keep her confidence."

"I looked up your Simon Kaplan."

"Oh, tell me. I'd almost forgotten."

"Clean or dirty, he's not in our database."

"Under the name Simon Kaplan."

"Right."

"I asked Marnie, when I talked to her this afternoon, if she had heard of him. She hadn't."

"Or said she hadn't." He parked the car and we got out.

"Goes without saying."

"Well, tonight we say good-bye to our son for a while."

"I'm not concerned," I said bravely. "He'll be fine." I wondered if I would. My son and I would be five thousand miles apart for almost a week. Thinking about it made me nervous.

"So will you," my prescient husband said. "I promise."

There were lots of hugs and kisses at dinner that night, and I handed my poor mother-in-law a list of things to help her around the house. She had visited enough times that she knew where I kept the silver and dishes and glasses, but I hadn't anticipated that she would have to turn up the heat and put the garbage out. The things we keep in our everyday memory amaze me. No wonder we sometimes think there's no room for anything else.

Eddie assured us he would show

Grandma how to do everything and I had a feeling he probably knew a lot more than I thought he did, although the temperature setting on the thermostat was beyond his height and knowledge. As long as he was warm, he didn't ask any questions.

Finally we said good night and got into our respective cars. I felt my eyes tearing a bit. I knew it was silly; I hadn't seen Eddie very much in the time we'd been here, but just the thought of all that distance between us rocked me a little. Jack must have suspected as much, because he put his arm around me as we went to the car and then held my hand as long as he could as he drove.

Tomorrow we were exploring the western part of the country. We still had one adventure left before our stay was over.

At twelve twenty-five on Friday I made a decision. At twelve-thirty I called Joseph. It was the early hour that bothered me. By this time she would have returned from morning prayers. I wasn't sure anyone would even answer the phone, but it didn't hurt to try. I listened to ring after ring and was about to hang up when a familiar voice answered.

"St. Stephen's Convent." It was a nervous-sounding Sister Angela.

"Angela, it's Chris. Forgive me for calling so early."

"Kix!" she said excitedly. "Are you calling from the Holy Land?"

"Yes, I am. I'm about to leave for a weekend trip. Is Joseph available?"

"Hold on. I'll get her. I just saw her go by."

I waited, hoping this wouldn't cost a fortune.

"Hello? Chris? Is that you?"

"Joseph, yes, it's me. I'm so sorry to bother you at this hour."

"Nonsense, I've been up for hours. You must have something important to tell me."

I told her quickly.

"Diamonds. Very interesting. I assume she hasn't told the police."

"She's afraid to. She thinks it'll look as though Gabe was involved in something illegal. She said he probably intended to use them to make a piece of jewelry for her."

"That's certainly a good possibility, although without seeing the gems we can't know if they're the kind you could use in a necklace or earrings, if there's a pair in the group, or if they're all different and meant to be held as an investment."

"I see what you mean. I've told you everything she said. When I get home, which won't be for another five or six days, I'll call her. She wants to talk to me in person."

"And she won't talk to the police."

"No. So I haven't told Jack what she found. He might be obligated to pass it on."

"Of course. I must say, I had no idea when I told you something might be put into the safe that this would happen. It's as much a surprise to me as I'm sure it was to you."

I told her what Jack had learned yesterday about the arrest of the two "ambulance attendants" and what they had said. "And that's about it. I think you know as much as I do today."

"The answers have to be at home," she said. "These people behind the murder knew Mr. Gross was going away — far away — for a week or so and planned this very carefully. What on earth did they put diamonds in that safe for, if indeed they did?" She was obviously asking herself the question. "Maybe they were hiding them there, Chris. Maybe someone was afraid the police were on to him and he didn't want the diamonds on his person or his property."

"Someone who worked for Gabe," I suggested.

"Or someone who knew him well but wasn't in the small group of best friends and relatives."

"OK, I have something to think about while we're touring this weekend."

"Just take lots of pictures and keep good notes. I look forward to a long afternoon with you when you get back. And you'll do the talking."

"I look forward to it, too. Have a good day." When I hung up, it was time to pick up Jack.

This time we drove west along the main east–west road from Jerusalem to Tel Aviv. When we reached Tel Aviv and the Mediterranean Sea we would turn north. I could see it clearly on the map. We would pass the airport where Eddie and his grandparents had left for home this morning.

"Funny to cross a country in an hour," Jack said as we drove.

"I can't even get to Albany in an hour," I said.

The beginning of the trip was more or less downhill from Jerusalem. When we eventually reached the point of turning north, we could see to our left the Mediterranean, a greenish sea with waves rolling onto the beach. I was surprised to find that most of the distance north was built up with apartment houses and businesses. For some reason I had thought the coast would be a continuous beach, but I could see how desirable it would be to live somewhere with a view of the sea, and I was not alone.

We reached Caesarea late in the afternoon and went in to see the ruins. I found I was very fond of ruins, and here we could walk among them, sit on them, touch them. We were even able to walk down to the sandy beach and pick up shells and small stones. I fulfilled my promise to Joseph by taking lots of pictures. In a shop I picked up some postcards to send home.

Mrs. Davidson had once again made hotel reservations for Jack and me farther north, and we reached the hotel happy and ready to eat. We had a fine dinner, took a long walk, and went up to our room to look at our maps and guidebook in preparation for tomorrow.

Saturday morning we continued our drive north. The Davidsons had told us there were several interesting things to see, one of them grottoes just at the Lebanese border, the northernmost point of our trip. We took a cable car down to the level of the grottoes and then started walking through them. We were right on the Mediterranean, the sea sweeping in, and as we began our walk a group of boys in their teens swam from the sea right into the grotto. We watched them from our walkway as they scrambled unsuccessfully to climb onto the slick steep rock across the inlet from us. I didn't think they'd make it, but suddenly one did, and he braced himself and helped pull the other two up. They congratulated one another heartily and started walking barefoot on the rocks, having saved the entrance fee and earned themselves an appreciative audience.

We drove south from there and turned east at the city of Nahariya, eventually arriving at a kibbutz where Rachel Davidson had a cousin. The cousin was expecting us and greeted us very warmly, taking us around the kibbutz to see the houses the families lived in, the dining hall, the farm animals, and finally a little shop that sold clothing made from Chinese silk hand-painted by members of the kibbutz. The colors were extraordinary and I selected some scarves for myself and as gifts.

"Get this for Mom," Jack said, holding up a scarf. "She loves reds and yellows."

We left with a bagful of beautiful things, thanked Rachel's cousin, and drove back to Nahariya, where we had a hotel reservation. In the evening we drove and walked through the city, admiring the homes that looked out on the sea.

"Too far for a vacation home," Jack said. "But nice, huh?"

"Very nice. I didn't know you had a vacation home in mind."

"I didn't till we came here. I like the smell of the sea."

So did I. A very nice smell.

We managed to find a Catholic church in Accho the next morning, thanks to Rachel's cousin's research. After mass, we visited Capernaum, walking alongside the foundations of the village built over two thousand years ago. We could see the small, wall-less rooms, the entries to the houses, the streets, such as they were, all of this built before Columbus set sail for the New World, before Leif Eriksson. The United States was settled two to three hundred years ago; here there were people living in communities thousands of years ago and the houses were preserved enough that we could see dirt floors and parts of walls and many artifacts, things they had used in their daily lives, like olive presses.

"I called Joseph before I picked you up Friday," I said to Jack as we walked along a dusty lane back to where the car was parked.

"About your call from Marnie Gross?"

"Yes."

"You're really making me jealous, Chris. You know I want to know what she told you."

"And you know I can't let you go to the police too soon."

"Somebody left something in the Gross safe."

"Yes."

"Let's see. Can't be a bomb."

"It isn't."

"Must be a letter. Somebody knew something or threatened something, maybe blackmail." I could almost hear his wheels turning. "But since her husband is dead now, the whole thing's moot."

"Could be," I said breezily.

"But it was important enough that you thought Sister Joseph should know."

"What I wanted her to know is that her suggestion was right, that someone might have put something into the safe, not taken something out."

"Seems like a very involved scheme to me. Why kill someone just to hide a letter in a safe five thousand miles away? It's overkill."

"Could be," I said again, equally breezily.

"You're a tough woman when you want to be."

"Well, you know those nuns who taught you in school."

262

"Don't remind me."

I just laughed.

We got back to Jerusalem in early evening. Jack had only two days left to work. Our long trip/vacation was nearing its end and I felt sad that we were leaving, disappointed that I hadn't made more progress on the murder. Jack was afraid he would have to work late on Monday just to be sure he got everything done by Tuesday. We were having dinner with the Davidsons Tuesday night, so Jack had to finish everything off by then.

"I keep thinking there's something in that database of yours that would help us in the Gabe Gross homicide," I said.

"There probably is. We just don't know what to look under."

"Simon Kaplan seems to have disappeared."

"Means you made him nervous."

"That works both ways," I said.

23

Simon Kaplan didn't show up again. On Monday morning I drove over to the hotel where the Gross family had stayed and walked around the lobby. I bought my *Herald Tribune* and planted myself in a visible spot, keeping the paper low enough that he would see my face if he walked through and glancing up frequently to look at passersby. No Mr. Kaplan. Finally I went to the front desk and asked the young man if he had seen someone of Kaplan's description. He hadn't. That didn't mean Kaplan hadn't been there, only that he hadn't been noticed by this particular person.

When I had done justice to the paper, I folded it, went out to the car, and drove away.

I spent the last two days visiting places I had missed and returning for a second visit to places I had enjoyed the first time. I had a good feeling of knowing the city, at least the part of it that Mel and Jack and I had driven through and wandered through. On Monday night Mrs. Davidson called and asked if I had visited Mea Shearim, the Orthodox section of the city. I hadn't gotten there and she offered to take me on my last morning.

She was an early bird, as I am, and at eight-thirty my phone rang and she said she was in the lobby. I went downstairs to find a young and very beautiful dark-haired woman waiting for me near the elevator. She introduced herself as Rachel and gave me a firm handshake. Then we went out to her car and drove.

She had warned me on the phone to wear something with long sleeves and no mini-skirt. I had smiled at that. I am not a mini-skirt person.

"You're dressed exactly right," she said as she pulled into a spot just vacated by a car the same size as hers. "The people here are very religious and the women are expected to cover up."

"What about in summer?" I asked.

"In summer, too."

"That must be very uncomfortable."

"I'm sure it is. But they do it."

We walked around and I saw young girls and women in their long sleeves and longish dresses in dark colors. Most of the men wore the little round caps that covered their heads. We passed a bakery where there was a line of women waiting to be served and a few feet from them a line of men. When I commented on it, Rachel said men and women did not touch each other and would not stand in the same line.

"This is really different from the rest of the city," I said.

"That's why I wanted you to see it."

"That's very kind of you. This is one of those places that shouldn't be missed."

"I have some time. If there's somewhere you want to go, I'll be glad to take you."

"I'd like to buy a present for my husband," I said. "But I don't know what. He's very hard to buy for."

"How about a silver key ring? I could take you to a place where they're handmade."

"I gave him one when he graduated from law school," I said.

"Your husband is a lawyer?"

"Yes. It took a long time, but he did it."

"It sounds like we're both married to very energetic men intent on moving upward."

I smiled. "Jack thinks your husband is very good at his job."

When she smiled back, I could see she was as proud of her husband as I was of mine. "Thank you," she said. Then, matter-of-factly, "Now, what about the present?"

"I wish I could think of something. He

doesn't wear rings; he has a fairly new wallet; he loves the key ring I got him —"

"Something religious?"

"He wears a silver cross that he's had most of his life." I thought a moment. "And a religious medal he's had for almost as long."

"Also silver?"

"Yes."

"Perhaps a chain to wear them on."

"They're on a chain."

"Come with me."

We drove to an unfamiliar part of the city, leaving me disoriented, and finally she parked in a lot and we got out and walked.

"This is Ben Yehuda Street," she said, "our walking street."

"Yes, now I know where we are. That's King George Street up there."

"You've learned our geography, I see. Come. There's a shop with a million chains."

She was right and I found one that I liked very much, just the right length and hand-made. After I asked the price, Rachel began to talk to the owner in Hebrew. It sounded slightly like an argument, but when she was done, the price of the chain had come down substantially and I realized she had been bargaining on my behalf. I kept quiet, paying for it in traveler's checks and thanking the man very much.

Outside I said, "What was that all about?"

"Oh, in that shop you must never pay the first price he asks. Only tourists pay."

"Well, thank you. I'll remember that on our next trip. I'm really glad you suggested this. It's a beautiful chain and I think Jack will like it very much."

She took me back to the hotel then. She was cooking dinner for us and had to get started. We were expected at seven, and while she cooked I had to pack my clothes and all the wonderful things we had gathered on the trip.

That evening was surely the best we had had on the whole trip. I wore the necklace of beads Jack had gotten me a week earlier and loved the way it looked. Jack insisted that Joshua call him by his first name, and reluctant as he was, he finally did. I felt better not hearing the respectful "Lieutenant" and "sir" every minute or so, and Rachel and I were already on a first-name basis.

Her cooking was wonderful. She was a Sabra, a native Israeli, she told us, born of parents whose parents had survived the Holocaust in Europe. She had recipes from her European grandmother and others from her

Israeli mother. And she offered us hummus as an appetizer before we sat down.

"I'm looking for a service that'll ship Chris a supply of that once a month," Jack said.

"Well, if Joshua gets his trip to the States next year, we'll take some along."

"Maybe Jack can pull some strings to make sure the trip happens," I said.

"Hey, why not? There have to be some perks to being a lieutenant."

It was a marvelous evening and we would have stayed later, but tomorrow was our flight home and Jack hadn't packed yet. Our farewells were warm and our invitations to them to visit very sincere.

Back in the hotel I decided I should give Jack his present, as we would have to declare our purchases when we arrived in New York. I didn't want any unpleasant surprises.

"I have something for you," I said when we got to our room.

"For me?"

I told him Rachel had taken me to a shop after our visit to Mea Shearim. The little box was in my purse and I handed it to him.

The result was more than I expected. "It's beautiful," he said, holding the chain across his palm and admiring the links. "I've always wanted a nice chain."

"You did? You never said a word."

"Well, you know me."

"It's handmade, Jack. Rachel insisted I not get one that was machine-made."

"It's great." He gave me a kiss, then another. "Really great. Would you believe I have something for you?"

"You mean you bought something while my back was turned?"

"Better than that. Take a look." He went to his suitcase and took a box out of the pocket along the side. "I hope it's what you want."

I couldn't imagine what it would be. The box was familiar, but I couldn't remember where I had seen it. I opened it, took away the soft cotton covering the contents, and gasped. Inside was the cross of Roman glass and silver Mel and I had seen at the wonderful jeweler at Hutzot Hayotzer. "Jack." I was stunned. "How — ? I can't believe this. It really is what I want."

"I figured. I knew you wouldn't tell me."

"Then how — ?"

"I gave Mel carte blanche. I said, 'Get whatever you think Chris wants most.' "

"Oh." I sat on the bed and just stared at it, feeling moisture in my eyes. "Thank you. Thank Mel. I am just speechless."

"There's a chain, too, by the way. It's in another box. I wanted you to see that first."

He gave me the second box and I found what was obviously also a handmade chain.

"I guess we really were made for each other," I said. "We gave each other almost the same gift."

"Yeah. Is this O. Henry's 'The Gift of the Magi' or something?"

"Something like that, but with a happier ending. How literary. How nice. How wonderful."

"Nice trip," Jack said. "Let's do it again."

In the morning, while Jack finished packing, I drove the car back to the car rental agency. It didn't take long to return it, and we saved Joshua the hassle. When it was done, I went outside and found a taxi.

"The American Colony Hotel," I said. "Please."

The driver took off and I realized the meter wasn't running. "Would you turn on the meter, please?" I said.

"I'll give you a good price. Twenty-five shekels."

"I don't want your price. Just turn on the meter."

"It's too late. We already went a kilometer. Twenty-four shekels."

I felt my heart pounding. "Turn on the meter," I said very sternly.

He flipped a hand at me in anger, an insulting gesture. I was fuming. I could feel my own anger mounting. I hated being treated this way, as though I were stupid, as though I were completely naive and he could put anything over on me that he wanted. I didn't know how to get him to turn on the meter, and I refused to ask him again.

He stopped at a traffic light, honked his horn at the car ahead of him for no reason I could determine, and muttered something in Hebrew. That's when I decided to do the only thing I could. I opened the door of the taxi, got out, and shut the door behind me. I crossed through traffic to the sidewalk, my hands trembling, my skin breaking into a sweat. I could hear him shout after me. Then the light turned green and he gunned the motor, still shouting, and continued down the street.

I calmed myself for a minute, then hailed another taxi, immediately asked him to turn on the meter, and gave him the address. In ten minutes I was back at the hotel.

24

When we arrived home, I felt almost light-headed, happy in a way I had never felt before. It was hard to believe this incredible trip had happened, that we had gone where we had gone, seen what we had seen. Eddie was glad to see us, and Jack's dad drove up to Oakwood to take his wife home so we wouldn't have to make the trip. We were five happy, contented people.

Jack had the rest of the week off, but he spent a lot of time on the phone with his office. I did the necessary shopping and Jack promised to cook through the weekend, as he was starting to feel rusty. He asked me to buy a can of chickpeas, and I had a good feeling about what that would turn out to be.

I called Marnie on Friday.

"Chris, I thought you'd forgotten."

"We needed a day to get back on schedule and get our clothes clean. But I'm available now."

"Please come here, OK?"

She gave me directions and I promised to

leave after lunch. It turned out she lived in New Jersey, not far from the George Washington Bridge. I hadn't been there since the first case I'd looked into, the murder of the mother of idiot savant twins back in 1950. I got involved in that one forty years after the fact but managed to find the killer and make a good friend while I was at it, Arnold Gold, a lawyer in Manhattan.

The Gross house was a few miles north of the bridge, and it was a magnificent residence. I turned into the private drive and parked near the house. The housekeeper opened the door and ushered me inside. As we walked toward the rear of the house, Marnie appeared.

"Chris, thank you for coming."

"How are you doing?"

"Nothing's easy." She led me to a small sitting room, and we sat at right angles to each other. She had closed the door when we entered, and now I saw why. She took a small gray pouch out of the pocket of her skirt. "This is what I found." She handed it to me.

I could feel the hard stones inside the pouch. "Have you touched them?" I asked.

"Several times. I checked every item in the safe, as you suggested, and this was one of them. And the jeweler I took them to handled every one."

That meant there were no prints on the stones that would be of use anymore. I opened the pouch. As Marnie had said over the phone, there were several wrapped diamonds inside. I opened one, the largest, and looked at it. I am no expert on diamonds or any other stone, but this one glittered with internal color. I held it up to the natural light coming in through the window and admired it. "It's very beautiful."

"And very real. It's worth — let me just say tens of thousands of dollars."

I rewrapped it and put it back in the pouch. "And you have no idea how they got in the safe or who put them there?"

"I have no idea who put them there, but I assume, if Gabe didn't buy them, that whoever broke into the house put them there. I just don't know why."

"I don't know, either, Marnie." I thought again of Simon Kaplan and asked if she was sure she had never heard of him.

"Positive. I called Gabe's secretary and asked her. She checked her Rolodex and all the files. His name didn't come up."

"He said he'd done business with Gabe."

"Chris, they don't throw files away. If he ever did business with Gabe, his name would be in some file or record somewhere."

"Then maybe he lied to me."

"Who is he?"

"If I knew that, I might know who killed your husband."

"This is so frustrating."

"My word exactly. It seems to me either he lied about having a business relationship with Gabe and his father or somehow that relationship has been deleted from Gabe's company."

She bristled at that. "Gabe was an honest man and an honest businessman. He didn't delete embarrassments."

"I'm sorry. I didn't mean to sound accusatory."

"Chris."

She was pressing her lips together, her face uncertain. I waited.

"There's one more thing."

"What do you mean?"

She reached back into the same pocket that had held the diamonds. "I found this on the shelf in the safe under the pouch." She leaned over and handed me a small piece of paper.

It was a note written in block letters with blue ballpoint. It said:

MARNIE, THESE DO NOT BELONG TO YOU. THE OWNER WILL

RECLAIM THEM. LEAVE THEM
WHERE THEY ARE AND KEEP
QUIET ABOUT THEM. <u>VERY
QUIET.</u>

The last two words were underlined. I realized she had known since the first moment she had talked to me about opening the safe that this note had been there. She had been trying to decide whether to tell me everything or just that she had found the stones.

"I wasn't sure whether to tell you," she said.

"Do you recognize the handwriting?" I asked.

"I probably know ten people who would write like that if they printed in capitals. Gabe could have. I could have."

That sounded about right. As I examined the writing, I felt I could have written it myself. "Someone is hiding the diamonds here."

"And I'm quite frightened."

"I think you have reason to be. He has a key to your house —"

"I changed all the locks," she interrupted, "and added some new ones, very big locks. I also changed alarm companies and had the system upgraded with new passwords and some new equipment. The safe combination was also changed. No one has a key to this house except me. And my lawyer, for the time being."

"That's a good idea. Whoever this person is, he can disarm the security system, but he can't get in the house without a lot of trouble. I think —" I stopped, not sure whether I should say what was on my mind.

"What?"

"Marnie, someone who knows Gabe well did this."

"I don't believe that."

I thought she looked a little tense as she said that. "I don't think that person is going to try to break into the house and the safe again. He knows you're smart enough to change the locks. He's going to come to you and ask for the stones back."

"How is that possible? Then I would know who killed Gabe."

"He doesn't care if you know. He has some reason not to fear a reprisal from you."

"How so?"

"Suppose it's Gabe's son," I said, pulling the first person out of my head. "He thinks you wouldn't go to the police because of his relationship to Gabe."

"But I would. I wouldn't let his son get away with murder."

"Maybe this person knows something that would keep you quiet."

"This is too complicated. It's outrageous. Gabe's son didn't kill him. Don't you understand? Gabe was generous to his children. This is crazy. This is just crazy." She took the note and the pouch and stuck them in her pocket. "I don't keep these in the safe anymore."

"That's a good idea. Marnie, why did you tell me this?"

"I thought you might see something that I've missed."

"I think I have. I think you have to sit down with yourself and make a list of people close to Gabe. Maybe one of them is running an illicit business. Maybe one is being paid off in stones instead of cash so there's no record of payment. Maybe the police are on to him and he wants to hide the stones where they're not in his possession. Marnie, this person knows both of you. He didn't address you as 'Mrs. Gross' in the note. He called you Marnie. He spelled it right, too."

"I know."

"So someone who knows both of you is involved. I think you know this person, even if you're not aware of it right now."

She looked down at the beautiful Oriental carpet at our feet. Then she faced me. "Are you done investigating, Chris?"

"I'm going to research the charities mentioned in Gabe's will. I sat on that plane the other day for more hours than I've ever sat before and thought about this. The former wife got a bequest. The children got money. You got the most, as you should have. Other people known to you got bequests. Then there are the charities. Did you look at the list?"

"Briefly."

"Anything stand out?"

"Gabe gave a lot of money to worthy organizations. We didn't discuss that. When we made out our wills, the ones he wanted remembered were listed. I have a different list, a smaller one, in my will."

"It's the only thing I can think of that I haven't checked out, that and the individual beneficiaries."

She stood, her right hand running down her skirt to reassure herself that the pouch was safely stashed. "You'll keep in touch?"

"Yes. One more thing. Do you have Gabe's lawyer's name and address?"

"I'll get it for you."

I waited for several minutes. When she returned, a piece of notepaper in her hand, I noticed that her skirt was flat again. She had put the pouch away somewhere.

"If you want to talk to him and he says

he's too busy, refer him to me. I'll see to it that you get a quick appointment."

"You'll hear from me," I said. "I promise."

When I got home, Jack was whipping up a storm in the kitchen. He shooed me away as he usually does and I went without reluctance. Anything he cooked for us would be better than anything I attempted. And I wanted to think.

I spread my things out in the family room, which is just off the kitchen. From there I could smell Jack's cooking and occasionally hear a syllable or two muttered under his breath, reassuring me that even the best of them make mistakes now and then. I took out Gabe's will and went over it again very carefully. A lot of it was boilerplate, phrases describing one's possessions, like furniture, clothes, cars, and so forth. I paid special attention to the individual names of people receiving bequests. The first ones were family, and they were dealt with generously. It was the ones on the second list that I looked at more carefully.

I didn't know who any of them were, and I hadn't asked Marnie. All of them had little descriptive phrases after the names: "the best friend a man could ever have," "more of a friend than an employee," "a secretary who earned more than I could give her," and so on. The secretary gave me pause. She was the one who couldn't find Simon Kaplan's name in the company files. But how could she benefit from Gabe's death? She probably didn't know he had left her a bequest. I have never heard of people going around telling their friends and employees that they'd been remembered in a will. Unless the diamonds would eventually go to her. And perhaps she knew something so damning about Gabe that when she claimed the diamonds, Marnie would not turn her in to the police. It was something to think about.

I decided to call the charities and inquire about the nature of their work and Gabe's relationship with them. Had he made an annual contribution? For how long? What was their mission?

I started with the largest ones, the most well known names on the list. I didn't get very far with them, and I wasn't surprised. "Records are private," "we cannot disclose," da-dah, da-dah. But I established that they existed at the addresses given in the will. I called what I assumed was Gabe's alma mater and couldn't get them to confirm even the year he graduated, but they did say he had been a student there.

One of the bequests was made to a home for abused women. The woman who answered the phone sounded harried and had never heard of Gabe, but she assured me they were at the listed address and that she was very busy and please call back another time. In the background I could hear voices and more than one baby crying.

I called what appeared to be a school for poor children and got an answering machine, which gave the school's hours as nine in the morning to four in the afternoon. I checked my watch. It was almost four.

By the time the business day had ended, I had checked most of the charities out and not learned a lot except that they all had telephones. When real people answered, they were forthcoming about their purpose, the people they helped, their goals. Most of them recognized Gabe's name, and several were aware that he had died tragically.

Jack's dinner was fabulous, which wasn't a surprise. And we started with hummus, as I had suspected. I told him it was every bit as good as what I had eaten in Israel and he grinned.

"I'll make an international gourmet out of you after all."

"You just may."

25

The following day I called the people on what I thought of as the second list of bequests. The man described as Gabe's best friend choked up when I talked to him about Gabe's death. He had been at the Bar Mitzvah and had left when Marnie did, although he and his wife had planned to stay for another week.

I reached the secretary at home. Her name was Flavia O'Rourke, and she sounded tense. "I know Mrs. Gross talked to you recently, Ms. O'Rourke," I said.

"She did, and I couldn't help her. There was no one by that name anywhere in my files, the man she asked about."

"I understand. I'm calling you because I'm trying to help find Mr. Gross's killer."

"Aren't the police working on it?"

"They are, in two countries. It's just that some suspects are in each country and it's hard keeping things straight."

"There are suspects?"

"There are people being questioned, let

me put it that way. I think the person who masterminded the killing is in the States."

"I wish I could help you. Mr. Gross was a wonderful man. I would have worked for him for the rest of my life. He was kind and generous and . . ." She faded off.

"There has to be someone who didn't feel that way."

"If I knew who, I would tell you. I would call the police. I would fly to Israel and tell the police over there."

"Are you aware that Mr. Gross has left you a bequest?" I asked.

There was silence. "You mean a gift?"

"A gift of money."

"I — no, I had no idea."

"He thought very highly of you."

"Thank you." I heard tears in her voice. "It was mutual, I can assure you."

Well, I thought, either she's a very good actress or she had nothing to do with it.

On Sunday, Jack and I got together with the Grosses — my Grosses, Mel and Hal. Mel described with relish how she had bought the Roman glass and silver cross for me, adding the chain that the artisan had made.

"It's so beautiful," she said. "I just love the colors."

"So do I. And you can't imagine how surprised I was. I couldn't figure out how Jack had known to get it or how he had gotten there."

"He planned it, Chris. I was in on it from the beginning. He's such a dear."

I told them what I was doing now, leaving out what Marnie had found in the safe. I still didn't want Jack turning over that information to the police.

"What do you expect to find out from those charities?" Hal asked. "I can't believe the UJA or the Red Cross would talk to you about a contributor."

"They won't, and I just called the big ones so I could cross them off my list. I thought maybe there'd be something fishy about the smaller ones, or about one of the individuals he left a bequest to. But every charity answered the phone or had a machine answer. One of them was a safe house for abused women, and I'm going to follow up on that. I could hear voices and children crying in the background. But what if it's a fake and someone's running it out of her home?"

"That's an interesting idea," Hal said thoughtfully. "You're thinking Gabe could have been seduced into making a bequest to what he thought was a legitimate, worthy organization that now turns out to be a fraud."

"Deceived," I said, a little chagrined at his choice of words.

"Of course," Hal said with a playful smile. "Deceived. So then this person who got Gabe to make the bequest decided to kill him before Gabe found out that the charity didn't exist."

"Exactly."

"How does the person know Gabe left them a bequest?"

I shrugged. "I have no idea. Maybe he told them. Maybe he let all these organizations know that he intended to give them a gift when he died."

"That happens. My alma mater encourages alumni to 'favor' the university in their wills and offers suggestions as to how to do it."

"So when you write asking for their brochure, they have a pretty good idea what your intention is."

"Right. I'll tell you, Chris, this is the best approach I've heard of. Maybe this will get you somewhere." Hal turned to Jack. "I think Chris may be on to something. I like her idea. Let us know about that shelter for abused women. If it turns out to be Mrs. Jones's home sweet home, I'd say you're on to something."

We stayed for cheese and drinks, then collected Eddie, who was upstairs with Sari and Noah, and walked down the street to our house.

"Hal seemed impressed with your idea," Jack said.

"Let's see if anything comes of it. It's only a good idea if it works."

On Monday I decided to visit the shelter rather than call. I had an address, which the woman on the phone had confirmed. Elsie Rivers, my mother's old friend and Eddie's surrogate grandmother on my side of the family, agreed to pick Eddie up at school. In fact, she couldn't wait. She hadn't seen him for almost a month, and she was looking forward to having him over. There might even be a baking lesson in the offing. I knew what that meant.

With that taken care of, I drove to the address in the will. It was in an old section of a town in New Jersey not too far from where Gabe had lived. I crossed the bridge and followed the directions Jack had worked out for me. The houses on that street were large and Victorian, some of them quite grand, others somewhat run-down. The one I was looking for was painted gray and badly needed to be scraped and repainted. I thought maybe a bright white or beige might help it look like a place to come home to.

I knocked on the door. A woman opened it only as wide as the heavy chain allowed. Perhaps, I thought, they were afraid angry husbands would burst in to reclaim the wives they had abused so badly that the women had felt it necessary to leave.

"Yes?"

"I'm Christine Bennett. I'd like to talk to whoever's in charge."

"You OK?"

"Yes, I'm fine. I'm not looking for shelter. I need some information."

She opened the door and reclosed it securely. "I'll tell Kim you're here. Christine Bennett?"

"Yes. She doesn't know me."

The woman trotted away. I stood in the foyer, waiting. A young pregnant woman carrying a toddler walked by, looking at me curiously. From not too far away I heard the kinds of sounds I had heard over the phone, crying, laughing, small children giggling and talking. I was pretty sure I had made a long trip for nothing.

"Ms. Bennett?"

"Yes, hello."

"I'm Kimberly West. Kim. We can probably find a corner to sit in in my office."

I followed her through a maze of hallways and rooms to a small office in a rear corner of the house. She sat on her rolling chair and I sat on the only other chair in the room, a wooden ladderback that had probably been swiped from a dining table.

"What can I do for you?"

"I believe Gabriel Gross made contributions to your shelter."

"Mr. Gross? Yes. Very generous contributions. I heard something . . . Is it true?"

"That he died? Yes."

"How awful. He was young and he seemed to be in very good health."

"He was. He was murdered."

She stared at me.

"Had he been contributing to the shelter for long?"

The phone rang and she excused herself, reaching for it across the desk. The conversation was short and monosyllabic. She dropped the phone back in its cradle. "You were saying?"

I repeated my question.

"About three years, I think. It could be more. I met him somewhere, a fund-raiser, I think, and buttonholed him. We always need money. We have more people here than we can sleep and feed. He was very sympathetic, asked for my card." She laughed. "If I spent money on cards, two people would miss out on dinner. Anyway, I got a check in the mail about a week later. A nice one. And there have been others since. Is there a problem?"

I admitted there wasn't and I thanked her for her time. I asked if I could use her phone to call New York and promised to pay for the call.

"I appreciate the gesture. Be my guest."

Someone somewhere was calling, "Kim? Kim, where are you?" She jumped up and left.

I called Gabe's lawyer's office and asked if I could talk to him in about an hour. The secretary said yes. I left a five-dollar bill for the call and took off.

"Mrs. Gross told me to expect to hear from you."

Harold Singer was about Gabe's age and graying. He gave the impression of being easygoing, but I assumed he could be tough as nails when he had to be. He knew what I had been doing, and if he felt at all skeptical about my abilities or thought I might be interfering, he kept it to himself.

"I understand from Mrs. Gross that there seem to be few leads to Mr. Gross's killer."

"That's what I understand. They have

two men in custody in Jerusalem, the men who kidnapped Gabe in a fake ambulance and probably killed him, but they haven't said anything that goes anywhere. They claim they don't know who they were working for and, of course, they didn't do the killing; someone else did."

"Someone else always does."

"Here's my idea." I sketched it out for him.

"I may be able to help you a little. I don't know the beneficiaries personally, but when Gabe gave me his notes I questioned him about each person."

"Do you have those notes?" I asked with hope.

"I doubt it, but I can look." He picked up a phone and asked someone to get the Gabriel Gross file. "As I recall, they were handwritten and as I made my own notes I think he crossed each name off the list so that nothing was left. He may have taken the notes with him or just tossed them in the wastebasket."

There was a knock at the door and a woman came in, dropped a file on his desk, and left without saying a word. He put glasses on and started looking through the many papers in the jacket, shaking his head as he turned the pages.

"His notes aren't here. In fact, I don't even see my notes." He frowned.

"You don't keep your original notes?"

"It depends."

Not much of an answer. "Everything look in order?"

He was holding the document that I assumed was the will itself. As I watched, he turned the pages, moving his index finger down each page from the top. "Looks in order to me."

"You said you might be able to help me with the beneficiaries."

"Yes, of course." He flipped a couple of pages. "These look like what he gave me. His wife, his ex-wife, his children." The finger moved across the page, back and forth. "Looks OK to me."

"And the other beneficiaries?"

"The big ones are well known. But Gabe had a soft heart. He would go to dinner with friends and someone in the group would have a special hobbyhorse, you know, something he was very interested in, dedicated to, and he would talk to Gabe. I'm sure some people lined up for the chance to be in the same room with him. If Gabe liked what he heard, he'd send a check."

"But these are sizable bequests."

"As I said, he had a good heart. Here's

one, this shelter for abused women in New Jersey. I'd say this place is marginally legitimate. They take in more women and children than they have beds and cribs for. Sometimes there isn't a lot to eat. But Gabe made them one of his own."

"How do you know this?" I asked.

"I actually took a drive out there when he put it in the will. I thought he might have been vulnerable to a request delivered with a sweet smile."

"I see."

"But they're on the up-and-up. They have the proper accreditation; they keep their heads above water. I'm sure his bequest will keep them going for a good long time."

"And the others on the list? Did you look into all the rest of them?"

"I didn't really have the time, and to tell the truth, Gabe didn't want me to. He knew who they were and he wanted them remembered."

"Did he ever change this will after he signed it?"

"No. I would know if he had. I haven't seen him for a couple of years although we spoke now and then. You don't look happy, Ms. Bennett."

"I don't like dead ends. Someone developed and executed a complicated plot to kidnap Gabe. Whether the murder was in the original plan or not I don't know, but it happened. There has to be something somewhere that gives me a lead."

"Some homicides go unsolved."

"I know, but I really want this one cleared up. I know several of Gabe's relatives and I've gotten to know his wife. She's devastated."

"Understandably."

"Mr. Singer, does the name Simon Kaplan mean anything to you?"

He pursed his lips and thought about it. "Can't say it does. I've probably met one in my life and forgotten him. He's not on the list, is he?"

"No." I described him and told Singer what had happened in Jerusalem.

"Can't help you, I'm afraid. I didn't know Gabe's father, and if Gabe ever mentioned this man it didn't stay with me."

I reached down to pick up my bag from the floor, where I had left it. "If someone had gone into your file and removed, say, your notes or Gabe's notes, would you have any way of knowing it?"

"No one went into that file without authorization, Ms. Bennett," he said testily.

"Well, I guess I'll just keep making my phone calls and hope to learn something useful. Thank you for seeing me."

He gave me a warm smile. "I'm glad you came down."

I offered him my hand and we shook. "If you think of anything —"

"Of course. I'll get in touch with you."

I left my name and phone number with the secretary and thanked her for arranging for me to see Mr. Singer so quickly. If something came up, she might remember I had been polite to her.

26

It was early evening when Marnie called. I had gotten back to Elsie's in the afternoon and spent an hour telling her about our wonderful trip. My narrative was frequently interrupted by Eddie, who had his own stories to tell. The one of his packing Dead Sea mud all over his body made Elsie laugh till she lost her breath.

"I hear you visited Harold Singer," Marnie said when I answered.

"Yes. I checked out a charity mentioned in the will and then I went to see him."

"Which charity?" Marnie asked.

"A home for abused women."

"Oh, yes, I remember that one. Gabe was very moved when he heard about it. They do good work there."

"It looks that way." I waited, wondering why she was calling.

"You know, Chris, I don't think what you're doing is going to go anywhere."

"Why do you say that?"

"I went through the list of beneficiaries and they all seem legitimate."

"That's what the lawyer said."

"And the charities — Gabe had so many he cared about. Whatever they do, he thought they were worthwhile, and it's not up to us to fault his judgment. You're not going to find anything there."

"So you're asking me to stop looking for his killer?"

"No, of course I'm not doing that. I'm just saying I don't think you'll find it by calling Gabe's secretary or his alma mater."

"OK," I said, not sure what she was suggesting.

"But if you do learn anything —"

"You'll hear from me."

I felt unsettled after our conversation. Why had she called? It seemed her intent was to tell me to stop looking into Gabe's death, but she had not wanted to say that in so many words. I have conversations from time to time in which I sense that the person I'm talking to is trying to get me to say what the caller doesn't want to say himself. It's as if it will come out better if it's my suggestion or my theory or my conclusion.

Marnie wanted me to back off the investigation. She knew something today that she hadn't known when I saw her last week. I opened my copy of the will and looked again at the list of beneficiaries, both individuals and organizations. The lawyer had pretty much vouched for the individuals, and they certainly seemed like people Gabe knew well. There were a few charities I hadn't contacted personally. Maybe if you could buttonhole Gabe at a party and get him to send a check, you might be able to deceive him about the work the charity did, although from what I had heard about Gabe, I thought he probably had someone check out these organizations before he gave them gifts. Tomorrow I would pursue the ones I wasn't so sure of.

When we were having coffee and Elsie's wonderful cookies after Eddie went to sleep, I asked Jack something that was bothering me: "If you were an estate lawyer and had made handwritten notes while talking to a client, would you throw out those notes after the will was finalized?"

"Hard to say. Since I'm not an old hand at being an estate lawyer, my instinct would be to keep them. They don't take up much room, a sheet or two of paper. But I can see tossing them when you don't need them anymore."

"I was just thinking that if there were ever any questions about beneficiaries, it might be helpful to go back to the original notes."

"Sure, and that's probably why lawyers

keep all that stuff. Someone objects to an heir getting so-and-so much, you go back and say, 'Look, here's what he said when he came to my office seven years ago.' "

"Gabe's attorney's original notes aren't in the file and I thought he looked a little uncomfortable about it. As if he thought they should be there and he was surprised they weren't."

"You saw him today?"

"I wanted to ask him about the people and organizations that are inheriting Gabe's money."

"And?"

"He looked over the list and thought everything was OK."

"But he didn't have his original notes to compare the will with."

"No."

"Could mean something, but I don't know what."

I left it at that. A couple of hours later, when I was walking up the stairs to our bedroom, something struck me. The note in Marnie's safe. Maybe she had figured out who had written it. And maybe she was afraid that if I kept poking around, so would I.

The next morning I called the teacher who had taken over my classes at the college and got a report on how things had gone. I had hastily e-mailed him, via Jack's computer at the Jerusalem police station, to ask him to fill in for one more class after we delayed our homecoming. He didn't seem at all bothered by the additional work and volunteered that teaching mysteries was a fun job.

I got my lesson together and then took the phone into the family room with my papers. There was something called the School of Good Friends that I had not reached the other day, so I called them now.

The woman who answered described herself as the secretary to the principal and said he could not be interrupted at the moment.

"Can you tell me a little about the school?" I asked.

I heard her expel air from her mouth in an annoyed manner. "Can I send you a brochure, ma'am?"

"I think I'd really like to see the school myself."

"Do you have a child who's planning to attend?"

"Not at the moment."

"We have very strict guidelines for our students."

"I would hope so," I said. "But I'm also interested in the school itself."

"I can give you an appointment next week."

If she was trying to discourage me, she was doing a good job. I didn't think I'd want my child in a place with someone like her in the front office. But as I was a person interested in whether the school had a building with classrooms and toilets, she was simply making me more suspicious by the minute. "Fine," I said. "How would Monday be?"

She turned a page. "Tuesday's better. Ten A.M.?"

"Thank you. I'll be there." I gave her my name, address, and phone number and hung up. Then I wrote a big red question mark next to the name of the school.

I then called the Double Eagle organization. For the second time, an answering machine responded. I didn't leave a message. Instead, I called Marnie. Perhaps she knew these two beneficiaries and could tell me something about them.

The housekeeper answered the phone. When I asked for Marnie, she said, "Mrs. Gross has left for a short trip."

"Oh." I was taken by surprise. "I just talked to her last night and she didn't mention that she was leaving."

"I'm sorry. She left about an hour ago."

"When will she be back?"

"I'm not sure. I can give her a message. She may call."

I declined her offer and hung up, feeling very uncomfortable. Something had happened. I had touched a raw nerve or Marnie knew who had put the diamonds in her safe or both. For all I knew, Marnie was home, having given instructions that she did not want to talk to me. Or she was away, perhaps to think over what she knew or suspected about the murder of her husband.

I looked at my watch. I still had most of the day ahead of me. I called Elsie, who had said she'd pick Eddie up at school, and I took off, armed with maps and addresses. My first stop was the School of Good Friends. This one was just north of the New York City border. I found the street and drove down it slowly, a residential street with people of different races walking themselves, their children, and their dogs. The school was on a corner, a brick building one story high with doors to each classroom. It was comparatively new and the grounds were clean, including a play area that contained equipment in happy colors for children.

I inched my way down the block and turned the corner to see the other face of the school. There were colored cutouts in many of the windows, and I could see children inside, some looking down at desks, some looking toward an invisible teacher. Satisfied, I found my way to the parkway and turned south toward the city.

The Double Eagle charity had an office in an old building on Tenth Avenue. I got off the West Side Highway at 79th Street and went down West End Avenue until I got to where I thought I was in the right area. East of West End most of the avenues are one-way and Tenth went north. I got on Tenth and found I had overshot a little, which was fine with me. I found a parking lot and left my car. I was getting hungry, having passed my usual lunch hour, but I decided to find the address before thinking about food.

The building was the usual five-story walk-up and I found a sign for Double Eagle on the ground floor, so at least I knew they really had an office, not a mail drop. I walked up to the third and found the door, which was locked. The name Double Eagle was painted on the wood in gold letters, but there was nothing else except the mail slot. I knocked and got no answer. I put my ear against the door and heard nothing.

I went down the hall to the next door and knocked, then opened it. Inside, a man in shirtsleeves sat at a messy desk, a bunch of papers in front of him and scattered all over the rest of the desk. He was holding a fat pen in one hand. Nearby was an empty crockery coffee mug.

He looked up at me. "You lookin' for me?"

"I'm looking for whoever works at Double Eagle."

"They don't come in much."

"Do you know their names?"

"Not offhand. It's a man sometimes, a woman sometimes. She's young. I guess he's young, too, if I think about it."

"And you don't know who they are."

"Never had the pleasure."

"Do you have the landlord's name?" I asked.

"You mean the guy we pay rent to?"

"Yes."

"I don't know if the landlord exists, but I send the rent to a box number. Wait a minute." He opened a drawer on the right-hand side of the desk and rummaged around. "E. Bolton Associates. That's who I make the check out to. But it's a box number. I don't guess he lives in that box."

"Probably not. Can I have the whole address?" I copied it down. "Do you remember the last time you saw this man or woman?"

"No idea. They owe you money or something?"

"Not exactly. They're inheriting and I have to check them out."

The man laughed loudly. "That's the oldest trick in the book, telling a guy he's got money coming so he'll give you his address and you can figure out his assets."

"In this case it happens to be true," I said, a little miffed at having been tarred with that particular brush.

"Well, good luck. I ever see them, I'll tell them you were lookin'."

I didn't think there was much chance of that, but I said, "Thanks," and went back downstairs. I stood on the street trying to think. They had an office and a telephone and an answering machine. Was there anything else behind that locked door? I had the image of a phone on the floor and an answering machine next to it. Was it possible?

Maybe I knew someone who could tell me.

27

The garage had a pay phone and I called my old friend Arnold Gold, the lawyer.

"Chris, you're back from Israel."

"I'm back and I'm at a pay phone and I don't have much change. Can I ask you a question and I'll talk to you from home?"

"Fire away."

"I'm trying to check up on a charity called Double Eagle. How can I find out the names of the principals? I've just been to the office and it's locked. I've called a couple of times and they answer with a machine."

"OK. Someone here worked for the Department of State where the charities register. Don't you guys have a computer yet?"

"The short answer is no. The longer answer is Jack's getting one any day now."

"You can find these things out when you get it, but I'll have an answer this afternoon and I'll leave it on your machine."

"Thanks, Arnold."

"We haven't seen you for a long time."

"Maybe this weekend."

"Sounds good."

The phone gave a warning click and we said our quick farewells. I paid for the car and headed home. When I got there, eventually, there was a message from Arnold on the machine. I called him back.

"Hello, Chris," he said jubilantly. "My right hand here has found your duly accredited charity, Double Eagle, on the Internet. The person who runs it is named Gary Helfer and the address is on Tenth Avenue in the big city, as you apparently know. I have no other information on him, but it looks as though he's in good stead. The purpose of the charity is to aid victims of Tay-Sachs disease. You know about that?"

"I've heard of it. It attacks children of a very narrow ethnic and geographical area."

"You are right on. It's Jewish children from Eastern Europe. If both parents carry the gene, there's a high probability the child will be born with it. Generally, these poor kids live only about three years and they're not very happy years."

I felt a chill pass through me. "It sounds like they do something good, but tell me, isn't there an organization to sponsor research for this disease?"

"I'm sure there is. These folks give assistance to the families."

"Is there a record of their having given such assistance?"

"There is. Not a lot of it, but I don't have the books in front of me."

"How long have they been around, Arnold?"

"Let's see. I think she's got it here. Yes. About three years."

"Three years."

"Are you in a position to tell me what you need this information for? Do I smell a homicide in your life?"

"A very sad one, Arnold. You know my friend Mel?"

"We've met. I think you told me you were going to be in Israel at the same time she was. 'A happy coincidence,' you said."

That sounded like me. I explained quickly what had happened, what we had learned, and where I now found myself, looking into beneficiaries to see if I could find a discrepancy in their claims or some hint of wrongdoing.

"This looks pretty clean," Arnold said after commenting at some length on the homicide.

"The office building is so shabby."

"Maybe that means they're spending very

little on administration and a lot on real charity. A lot of organizations don't, you know."

"I've heard. The problem is they don't seem to be there. The man down the hall barely knows who they are."

"Maybe they come in to pick up the mail and write the occasional check."

"It bothers me."

"I know you want me to say they look dirty and maybe you've found what you're looking for, but I can't. Ask Jack to look up this guy Helfer. Maybe he'll find something."

"I'll do that. Thanks, Arnold."

"And the invitation for this weekend is solid. I called Harriet and she said you should come."

"I'll have an answer for you after I see Jack tonight."

"Make it a good one."

I laughed. I was sure Jack would say yes. Jack and Arnold had become increasingly close as Jack finished law school, took the bar exams, and started to do legal work for NYPD. I think of Arnold as my surrogate father, but he's been almost that to Jack in some important ways.

I gave Jack the name of the supposed administrator of the charity that evening, and he promised to check up on it the next day. Wednesday was my teaching morning, so I didn't have much time for anything else. My students all appeared rather glad to have me back, and I wondered if my replacement had run a tighter ship than I, but I wasn't about to ask.

We had a good class, which started a bit late, as they seemed really interested in my trip, or perhaps they thought the delay was in their best interests. When you teach, you can't help thinking such things. We were coming to the end of the fall semester, and we spent most of the class reviewing the books we had read and analyzed since September. At the end of the class, several students came to ask my advice on the term paper I had assigned, and I stayed on to talk to them. When we were all done, I had my usual good lunch at the college cafeteria and bought an apple pie, still warm and smelling temptingly of cinnamon, to take home for the rest of the family.

I found a message on the machine for me to call Jack, and I did rather eagerly, hoping he had some information on Gary Helfer.

"Hit pay dirt," Jack said.

"He's got a record?"

"Yup. Small-time stuff, but running a fake charity looks to be just up his alley. I tried

311

the phone number you gave me and got the answering machine again. Guess he doesn't spend much time in his office. But I've got a home address for you."

"That's great." I reached for a pencil and the back of a used envelope. "OK."

"You can't go alone, Chris. I'm really nervous about this guy. He could be the killer. Either I'll go with you or I'll get someone on the job to go. And I've got something else here. What was the name of that old guy you talked to a couple of times?"

"Simon Kaplan."

"He's on the board of directors."

"Simon Kaplan knows Gary Helfer?" I felt a little dizzy. "He told me he was a friend of Gabe Gross."

"People have been known to lie, dear wife."

"That's some lie. He's one of the bad guys, not one of the good ones."

"Could be. But remember, you haven't established anything yet."

"No, but when something like this happens, I get a good feeling that things are coming together."

"Exactly why I don't want you going to Helfer's house alone. I'll bring everything I have home for you to look at."

"Jack, there has to be a connection between this Gary Helfer and Marnie Gross. I think she's sorry she told me what she did —"

"What you didn't tell me."

"Right. And she's left town. Or so her housekeeper says."

"Interesting. Why don't you ask Hal what Marnie's maiden name is?"

"Just what I was thinking."

I couldn't do it right now because Mel was teaching and she wouldn't come home for a couple of hours. So I sat down and corrected the exercises my class had turned in and worked out my lesson plan for next week. By that time everyone was coming home from school and I had cleared my desk.

"Good question," Mel said. We had walked over to her house. "Mind if I ask you why you want to know?"

"A name has come up and I want to know if there's a connection to Marnie."

Mel looked distressed. "Marnie's OK, Chris. Really."

"I didn't say she was involved. Do you know her maiden name?"

"I think it was something like Gilbert. Yeah. That sounds right."

"You sure?"

"I'll ask Hal when he comes home. He'll remember. But I remember meeting her the first time and Gabe called her Marnie Gilbert. Is that good or bad?"

I laughed. "Bad, actually. I was hoping for something else, but let's see what Hal says."

We left it at that and talked about other things till it was time for both of us to get dinner ready. In the evening, I looked at the material Jack had brought home. There, in black and white, was the name Simon Kaplan. Simon Kaplan was or had been a diamond dealer, and diamonds had been found in Marnie's safe. Had she lied to me about knowing him? Was it possible she was in on the murder of her husband? I hoped not. It wasn't the kind of thing I wanted to discover.

Hal called about nine o'clock. "You wanted Marnie's maiden name?"

"Yes."

"I don't know it. Gilbert was her married name."

"She was married before Gabe?"

"Definitely. Tell you what. I'll research it for you tomorrow. I know where she was married and I can find out. In order to get married in New York State when you've been married before, you have to show

proof that you're divorced or that the marriage was annulled."

"So her maiden name should be on the
record."

"Should be. I'll find out tomorrow."

28

I was actually fidgety the next morning, waiting to hear from Hal. I kept turning over in my mind what I would do if he said Marnie's name was Smith and what I would do if it was Helfer. Of course, even if it turned out to be Smith or Jones or a thousand other names, that didn't rule out a relationship between her and Gary Helfer, blood or otherwise. The "otherwise" type of relationship could be just as strong. Lots of people have committed heinous acts for people they loved and to people they hated with no blood or legal relationship between them.

The call came finally after I had had my traditional lunch of tuna salad on a nice roll with a glass of tomato juice and the *New York Times* alongside my plate, rather wishing my lunch was hummus and pita bread and fresh tomatoes.

"Chris," Hal said, "I've got an answer to your question."

"I can't wait to hear."

316

"Marnie Gilbert's maiden name was Helfer." He spelled it out.

"Hal, I can't thank you enough."

"Did I hit the jackpot?"

"You sure did. It's the name I was looking for."

"You're not telling me Marnie was involved in Gabe's death."

"I don't know. But someone she knows may have been."

He whistled. "That's a shock."

"We should know pretty soon. Thanks again."

I got back to Jack.

"No kidding," he said. "You got a match."

"It must be her brother, or maybe a cousin."

"OK. This guy lives at a Manhattan address. I'd guess it's an apartment. When do you want to go there?"

"What do you think, day or evening?"

"I guess evening's better. He may work during the day."

"Is that a joke?" I asked.

"In this case, it probably is. Let's see what I can work out for tonight."

I thought it best not to tell Mel what I had learned. Late in the afternoon, Jack called and asked me to see if Elsie could come over and baby-sit, so I knew he

317

wanted to join me. I also knew he would alert the Manhattan detective squad in Gary Helfer's precinct and at least one detective would surely accompany me to the apartment. And Jack had probably called the Special Frauds Squad to alert them about a possible charity scam, which would add another detective. I hoped it wouldn't be overkill.

I got together a quick dinner and told Eddie that Elsie would be staying with him for a while tonight.

"Can I come with you?" he asked.

"We won't be back till late, honey. You'll get very tired."

"Can I come next time?"

I rumpled his hair. "We'll see when next time comes."

Jack got home a little early, and we sat down to eat right away. When we were done, Jack took care of the dishes while I dashed upstairs to give Eddie his bath. Elsie showed up right on time and I put some lipstick on, gave Elsie a hug and Eddie a kiss, and Jack and I drove into New York.

Helfer's apartment was off Park Avenue in the low Nineties, the Two-Three, and we had some trouble finding a place to park. The streets were lined with cars, but we found a garage about a block away. Helfer's building was old, built before people realized that cars came with tenants, before garages were mandated in new construction. Although it was old, it was beautifully kept, the lobby refurbished, the doorman in a spanking uniform. The elevators were obviously new and moved silently and swiftly.

Two Manhattan detectives, one from the Twenty-third Precinct, one from Special Frauds, were waiting for us outside the building when we got there, their car discreetly parked elsewhere. Their names were Monaco and Flowers and they remained downstairs while we went up, in order to be certain the doorman did not announce that the police were coming. They said they would follow us up and remain outside the apartment till they were called.

I rang the bell and waited till an eye appeared at the peephole and a woman asked who was there. I gave her my name, and she opened the door. The doorman had said there was no Mrs. Helfer but that a woman was often in the apartment. Doormen know everything.

She opened the door and I asked to see Gary Helfer.

"He'll be back in about five minutes. Can I ask what this is about?"

"About the Double Eagle charity."

"Come in." She was younger than I, in her late twenties, I thought, and quite good-looking. She was wearing the kind of clothes I don't even dream about wearing, a silk pants outfit in fiery shades of orange with a golden scarf that must have been light as a feather, the way it moved when she did.

I stepped inside, leaving Jack in the hall. "Thank you. I hope I'm not intruding."

"Not at all. If it's the charity you're interested in, there's someone here who can talk to you."

"Oh?" I wondered if I had understood her correctly.

"Just a moment and I'll get her." She left the room and I remained standing, feeling a bit confused. The living room I was in had a beautiful floor that looked new and well polished. The furniture was striking, fine woods, and the area rugs seemed too good to step on. I started wondering where the money had come from.

"Here she is."

I turned and stood face-to-face with Judy Silverman, Gabe Gross's daughter.

"Chris," she said, as shocked as I was. She looked a little frightened, as though she wanted to get out while she still could.

"Judy. You're part of Double Eagle?"

"It's — yes, it's a charity. I give a lot of time to it."

The silk-clad woman looked confused. "You know each other?"

"We've met," both Judy and I said almost in unison.

I went to the door and opened it. Jack was right there. "He's not here. He's supposed to be coming back any minute. I'm surprised the doorman didn't say anything."

"Maybe he took a break." Jack came inside.

"This is Judy Silverman, Jack," I said. "Gabe's daughter."

Jack nodded. "Ms. Silverman, I'm Lieutenant John Brooks, NYPD."

Judy's face paled. "What are you doing here?" Her voice was shaking.

"We want to talk to you and Mr. Helfer."

"About what?"

"About the charity, Double Eagle, and a few other things."

"What other things?" Judy asked, her voice hard.

At that moment I realized the other woman had left the room. "Jack, his girlfriend may be warning him."

Jack opened the door and spoke to the detectives who were standing in the hall. They moved quickly toward the elevators.

Then Jack came back in. "Where is she?" he asked Judy.

She shrugged.

"Where did Helfer go?"

"For a run. He's bringing back something to eat."

There was a buzz and Jack said, "Is that the doorman calling?"

"Maybe," Judy said.

Jack found the kitchen and picked up the intercom. "OK, thanks," I heard him say. He came back. "He dropped a bag of Chinese take-out on the lobby floor and ran. The cops took off after him."

"I don't understand what's going on," Judy said.

"You'll understand soon," Jack said.

About five minutes later the detectives rang the doorbell and came inside with a man in running clothes. There was no Chinese food to be seen.

"What the hell is this all about?" Helfer said angrily as the detectives released him.

"Sit down and let's talk," Jack said.

"I want my lawyer."

"You haven't been charged with anything."

"I don't give a damn. I'm not talking without my lawyer."

"Then call him. He can meet you down at the station house."

Helfer looked at both of us. Then he almost smiled. "Officer," he began in a calmer voice.

"Lieutenant," Jack corrected him. "Lieutenant John Brooks."

"I'm sorry; no insult intended. Lieutenant, I'm sure we can work something out here. What exactly do you want from me?"

"We need information on the Double Eagle charity."

"Hey, if that's all this is about, why didn't you say so? My books are open to the public. Would you like to see them now?"

"I'd like to take them with me. You'll be given a receipt."

"It's too extensive, sir. I have file cabinets."

"We can carry the files."

"Please come into my office."

We followed him into a beautiful large room with a fine desk, a thick carpet, and an exercise machine near the window. He had a single file cabinet, which he opened to show Jack the contents. There really weren't a lot of file folders in each drawer. Each of us carried one drawerful out, and Jack gave Helfer a receipt.

"Where is your list of contributors?" Jack asked.

"It's under 'C.' "

"I'll be in touch."

★ ★ ★

"We're going to lose him," I said when Jack and I had finally gotten into our car.

"I have nothing on him, Chris. There are circumstantial indications that he's involved in Gabe's death, but nothing I can consider evidence."

"He ran when he saw the detectives."

"He panicked. Lots of people do. It doesn't mean they're guilty."

"We'll never see him again," I said. "He'll be gone in the morning."

"I don't think so. He's got to stick around for that check from Gabe's estate. It's seven figures. It's what he's been waiting for."

I waited a moment before saying what was on my mind. "The purpose of this evening was for me to talk to Gary Helfer. I ended up a minority of one with two detectives and a lieutenant. I didn't get a single word in."

"You're annoyed."

"I guess I am. I was a tagalong at a police show. And it was a disaster."

"I couldn't let you go alone."

"I shouldn't have gone at all. None of us should. We've tipped our hand. Both Helfer and Judy Silverman know we're suspicious of the charity."

324

"They can't move without that check, Chris."

I had said my piece.

"Let me tell you what Marnie found in her safe," I said when Jack and I were home and I had cooled off. I told him quickly. It needed no embellishments.

He whistled when he heard it. "And you figured someone she knew left them."

"Eventually I decided that this Gary Helfer was being looked at for another crime and he didn't want the diamonds in his possession."

"I will check that out tomorrow. You think Marnie knows he left the diamonds?"

"I think she realized it after she showed them to me. That's why she called and said she didn't think it was worth my working on it anymore."

"Let me ask you something. Do you think Gabe really wanted to give Helfer's charity a few million bucks?"

"I think Gabe was too smart to do that. I just can't figure out how Helfer got Gabe to put that in his will."

"Well, let's sleep on it. And let's hope we come up with something in those files, although I'm afraid we won't. If Helfer and Gabe's daughter are involved in a swindle that included homicide, they're probably running that charity as clean as new snow."

"They're taking money off the top, Jack. That's how he can afford that apartment and all the expensive furnishings."

"And the expensive companion."

I smiled. "How do you think I'd look in a silk outfit like hers?"

"Intimidating. I'd be afraid to touch."

"OK. Then I won't get one."

"Good thing. I'd need at least a captain's salary for that."

First thing in the morning I drove to Marnie's house without calling first. The housekeeper recognized me when she answered the door and thought a moment before calling Marnie. When Marnie saw me, she stopped cold.

"I only have a minute," she said.

It was a much less inviting greeting than the last time I had been here. "That's all I need, Marnie. Your brother is Gary Helfer."

She froze. "What does that have to do with anything?"

"He left the diamonds and the note in your safe."

"That's not true."

"Think about it, Marnie. Think about

what that means. He may have ordered Gabe's murder."

Her eyes brimmed with tears. "My brother wouldn't do that. My brother is a good person. He's had some problems, but he's gotten over them."

"I'm sure you love him very much."

The tears began to fall. "Our parents died when I was in my teens. He took care of me. There wasn't always enough money, but he managed. I owe him my life."

"I understand, Marnie. But your husband's life was just as valuable and your husband loved you."

"I know." It was a whisper.

"I think you know what you have to do."

"I can't. I'm sorry. Please go."

As I left the house, two policemen got out of a car and walked up to the front door. One of them was carrying a search warrant.

29

When I got home there was a message on the machine: "Ms. Bennett, this is Elaine, Attorney Singer's secretary. Please call me when you get back."

I called immediately.

"Ms. Bennett, good morning. Mr. Singer and I were talking yesterday and I reminded him that we had a break-in about two months ago."

"Was anything taken?"

"A few dollars of petty cash in my drawer and my typewriter. I don't know why anyone would steal a typewriter nowadays."

"It does seem odd," I agreed.

"We reported it to the police and they tried to lift prints, but it looked like a professional job."

"And that's all they took?" I said, trying to see where this was going.

"There was one peculiar thing. I don't know if it has anything to do with the break-in. I always pull the plug on the printer before I go home. Something happened once and now I do that every night. When I came in the next morning and went to plug it in, the plug was already in the strip. Oh, just a minute. Mr. Singer wants me."

A moment later she had connected the three of us in a conference call. Harold Singer gave me his take on the burglary.

"It was small-time," he said. "They did it for beer money. These things happen in Manhattan. Thank heaven nothing was destroyed and they didn't trash the office."

I asked him if he could take a look at his copy of Gabe's will. "Elaine told me someone had plugged in her printer. I'm wondering whether that means something."

"Elaine, can you find Gabriel Gross's will?" he said.

"One moment."

As we waited, I could hear him tapping a pen on his desk. Maybe this was it, I thought. Maybe this was the thing that could link everything.

"OK, here it is."

"Would you turn every page and see if they all look the same?"

"OK."

I waited, hoping he would find something.

"They look the same to me."

"Are the pages initialed?"

"Yes."

"Would you check the initials?" Again I waited. I needed something. I didn't want a killer to go free.

"Well," he said, "there's one page where the initial could be slightly different. Not much. Maybe I'm just looking too hard. It almost looks as though it was done with a different pen, a slightly thicker point."

"What's on that page, Mr. Singer?"

"Part of the list of charities he was endowing."

"Mr. Singer," now my heart had picked up its beat, "is Double Eagle on that page?"

"Yes. Here it is. Near the top."

"How easy would it be for someone to produce a page of the will using your computer?"

"Very easy," Elaine said. "Just use my word-processing software, which is what I use most of the time, and print it out using the same font."

"So someone could change one item or line or several lines and print it out and you would never know the difference?"

"Well, it has to be initialed."

"And if the same pen wasn't around?"

"I see what you're saying." It was the lawyer now. "It's easy to copy an initial, isn't it? And if you used a different pen, it might be a little thicker or thinner or darker or lighter."

"Exactly."

"I see your point," he said. "Someone may have added a listing. They'd probably have to subtract one to make it fit, and without my original notes I can't tell you if anything is missing. Or if anything has been added. But it's a good theory, and it may be what happened. Still, I have to tell you I have a 501.3(C) for them. They're a legitimate tax-exempt charity."

Legitimate, I thought, meant only that the government hadn't dug deep enough. "Tell me, Mr. Singer, when do you anticipate sending the checks for the bequests?"

"They went out today," Elaine said.

"Today?"

"The mailman came about ten this morning and I gave him the outgoing mail. All the checks were there."

"So there's a good chance they'll be delivered in Manhattan tomorrow morning."

"I would hope so. And you know, someone called from Double Eagle last week to ask when the checks were coming."

"Ms. Bennett." It was the lawyer's voice. "Tell you what I'll do. I'll put a stop on the Double Eagle check and I'll notify the charity that an irregularity has come up. You've raised some uncomfortable questions. But I have to warn you, if you don't come up with something definitive in forty-eight hours, I'll have to issue another check."

I got the point.

When I got off the phone, much as I didn't want to make the trip again, I drove back to Marnie's house. Elsie had been enlisted to take care of Eddie, so I had the time.

"Chris," she said when I came in. "Did you call the police to come here?"

"No, I didn't. There's an investigation into Gabe's death and I expect one of the detectives did that."

"You told them about the diamonds."

"Last night. I kept it a secret until then. But last night I couldn't keep it a secret anymore."

"They took them, the diamonds. I don't know whose they are or what they're worth, but I guess they're not mine anymore."

I didn't comment. "Marnie, did your brother ever meet Gabe's daughter?"

"Funny you ask. They did. How did you know?"

"Just a thought. How long ago was it?"

"It was just after we were married, about

three years ago. We gave a party and invited a lot of people, friends of mine to meet Gabe, friends of his to meet me. Judy came and my brother came. I knew she didn't like me. I'm a lot younger than her mother and she always had it in her head that Gabe cheated on her mother with me. She never came again when we invited her, and she and Gabe had no real relationship.

"But that night I remember seeing her talking to Gary. They talked a lot. I was surprised. I hadn't thought about that for a long time."

"Marnie, did Gabe keep a file on the information he gave Harold Singer for his will?"

"I'm sure he must have. He was a very organized person. I suppose you want to see it."

"Please."

She took me into her husband's study, a small, pleasant room with a lovely view of the grounds behind the house. The file cabinets were built in and she looked in several places before pulling out a folder.

I sat in a chair, not wanting to use Gabe's desk, and opened the file. There was a draft of the will with a number of things crossed out and other lines and phrases inserted. He had certainly worked on this document himself. Behind it were pages of handwritten notes and scraps of paper with phrases, questions, and dates.

I looked through the draft of the will first. There were no charities listed, just an almost empty page where he had written: "Bequests to Charities." But the list was spelled out in his own handwriting. I read through it twice, running my finger down the pages as Harold Singer had done when I saw him in his office. There was no Double Eagle.

"What is it you're looking for?" Marnie asked. "You've seen the will."

"There's a discrepancy," I said. "May I take this folder with me?"

"I suppose if I don't give it to you, you'll have the police come and take it."

I didn't say anything.

"Take it. What difference does it make anymore? I can assure you my brother isn't mentioned anywhere in Gabe's will."

"I know that," I said.

"Then what's the point?"

"I'll explain it to you, but not today."

"I think I don't even want to know."

I let it be.

30

I waited till Eddie was off to bed to tell Jack. I had the folder with Gabe's notes on my lap and my copy of the executed will.

"There's no Double Eagle in the notes," he said.

"Right. And if you look at the notes, here's a charity that's missing from the final will."

"So your theory is Helfer and Judy deleted one charity at the bottom of the page and inserted Double Eagle alphabetically near the top."

"That's exactly what I think."

"It's a good theory. How do the diamonds fit in?"

"The diamonds were an afterthought. They're a payoff to him or something like that, and he was afraid that wherever he hid them, they'd be found. But they wouldn't be found in his brother-in-law's safe. So when he went to substitute this page of the will, he left the diamonds there, expecting to retrieve them later. Helfer and Marnie are very close. He knew she would never believe he was involved in killing Gabe and even if she did, she wouldn't be able to turn him in."

"Sounds good to me. Now how do you connect Helfer and the daughter?"

"They met at a party. Marnie told me about it. It was soon after she and Gabe got married. They must have recognized each other as kindred spirits. He saw a way to make money; she saw a way to hurt her father. I expect they hatched the plan soon after."

"That's some story."

"And the checks to the charities went out at ten this morning. They may be delivered tomorrow. We really have to move."

"OK. Let's draw up a plan."

The plan was simple. We would pick up Helfer when he came for his mail. Elaine had said at the end of my conversation with her and the lawyer that the recipients had been notified that the checks had been sent. Helfer wasn't going to let that check sit on the floor of his office any longer than he had to. He wanted it turned into cash as soon as possible. If Judy showed up with him, and I assumed she would if he had told her the check was coming, we would have her, too. In the meantime, Jack had an old mug shot photo of Helfer from a previous arrest faxed to Joshua Davidson in Jerusalem. They would make a photo array and show it to the men in custody for identification. With the time difference, we would have an answer before the start of our workday tomorrow.

In fact, we had the answer before Jack left for work. Joshua called us at home. One of the men refused to say anything; the other identified Helfer as the person who had commissioned the kidnapping. He still refused to admit he had anything to do with Gabe's homicide, but we had an ID. I was almost jumping for joy.

"That's good," Jack said when he got off the phone. "And Joshua and Rachel send you their best regards. I think you made a hit with both of them."

"So did they with me."

We went into the city in two cars so I could get back after the arrest. And I wanted to see Eddie off to school. After today, I hoped, I would have time to take a break and spend some time where my heart was, with my family.

I actually found a place to park on the street and I met Jack where he was parked, down the block from the entrance to the Double Eagle office building, if you could call it that. Two detectives I hadn't seen before were there, too, and the cops in the sector car had made their check of the building, one of them remaining out back to be certain no one made a dash that way.

The mailman showed up a few minutes after I arrived and went inside. I knew he would be in the building awhile, as the doors to the offices all had mail slots. I was right. It took him more than ten minutes to come back outside.

The cops were well hidden, including Jack, who was one door away from the entrance. I sat in my car watching the sidewalk for Helfer. He must have had a good idea when the mail arrived, because he showed up just as the mailman was leaving. I assumed he had been waiting down the block. As he passed my car at a good pace, I got out and followed him.

Jack emerged from his doorway as I got there, and we walked toward the door Helfer had disappeared through. I wondered if he already had a plane ticket to some wonderful place where he hoped to spend the next many years. He would have to make a stop at a bank, I thought, unless he had an account somewhere else that the check would go into. Neither Judy Silverman nor the apparent girlfriend from the other night was anywhere to be seen.

I waited nervously near Jack, wondering if Helfer would go out the back way when he came down. The detectives were on the far side of the doorway. I know it didn't take all that long, but it seemed to. Finally, Gary Helfer walked out to the street, his head down as he looked over his mail.

"Don't move, police," one of the detectives said.

Helfer was as surprised as anyone I have ever seen. "What?" he said.

"You're under arrest for the murder of Gabriel Gross in Israel and for fraud in the state of New York."

"I don't understand, Officer," he said, clutching his mail and looking at the shield thrust in his face by the detective. I could see him on the verge of running, his legs tense and starting to lean away from the detective, but he must have changed his mind.

The detective cuffed him, taking the mail from his hand over his objections. The group stood on the street just long enough for the detective to recite the litany of the Miranda warnings to Gary Helfer. His grunts were duly noted as "yes" to each part.

Then Jack confronted him. "Where's Judy Silverman?"

"How should I know? I want a lawyer right now!"

"Do it," Jack said to me, and I took off with the second detective, Kevin McHugh, for Judy's address, which Jack had given me last night.

"What are you talking about?" Judy Silverman asked.

I was in her living room in the apartment she shared with her husband, who wasn't there. Outside the door, Detective McHugh was waiting for trouble or to make an arrest. He had given me an alarm I could squeeze in case I sensed danger. What I wanted was a confession. They'd never get one from Gary Helfer. I had just told Judy that Helfer had picked up the bequest check for Double Eagle. She looked blank.

"Didn't he tell you?" I asked.

It was obvious that he hadn't. "I don't know what check you mean."

I tried to assess her veracity. "The reason Gary broke into your father's safe. The reason your father was murdered."

"I don't know why they killed my father. All they were supposed to do was get the key to the house and the combination. Gary was going to steal Marnie's jewels and the cash my father kept in the safe. He kept a lot of

340

cash there. They were supposed to let my father go as soon as Gary got into the safe."

"Who told you about the cash and jewels?"

"Gary did. He heard it from Marnie after she married my father."

"And you believed him."

She stared at me, saying nothing.

"What about the charity?" I asked, not wanting to give away something that she might not know about. "Double Eagle."

"What about it? Gary started it up. It did a lot of good and he was able to use some of the money to improve his lifestyle."

"And the will?" I said. Was it possible she didn't know?

"What about the will?"

I think that was when I realized she didn't know what Gary had done. He had let her in on only part of the plan. "Was Gary going to share the proceeds with you?"

She nodded, still looking confused.

"He was arrested about half an hour ago."

"I see."

"Did he give you any of the money and jewels?" I knew none had been taken, but it appeared that she didn't.

"Not yet. He was waiting for something, he said, something to come in the mail. I suppose I won't get it now. It doesn't matter. I didn't do it for the money."

And there was her admission that she had done it, that she was in on it. "What did you do it for?"

"To teach my father a lesson. To make him hurt. He wasn't supposed to die, you know. I'm not a killer."

"Gary left some diamonds in the safe," I told her. "What can you tell me about them?"

"Gary's involved in certain businesses that don't pay in cash. He was paid in diamonds for something he did and the diamonds were traced. I think Interpol was involved. He was afraid they'd find them, so he put them in my father's safe. Marnie would never turn him in. At least, that's what he thought."

"She didn't," I said. "How did he intend to get them back?"

"Get them out of the safe when he visited her sometime. They're pretty close. He could have done it. If that didn't work, he would ask her for them. He had a story ready. Gary always has a story ready."

"But then she would know he had ordered the killing of your father."

"He had a story ready for that, too. Gary is very resourceful. He's a clever man. This was all his idea. I met him at a party and told him what I thought of my father. He picked up on it and called me a week later. He wanted to wait until my father gave Marnie some special jewels and they would be out of the country for some time. This turned out to be the right time."

It was strange hearing this young woman brag about her good deeds when she had just admitted to being in on a murderous plan with her own father as the victim.

"You worked on this plan for a long time."

"Since they married. I was very distressed when you found out I was at that hotel. I was there to make sure everything went the way it should. It did, you know. Except that my father died."

"Who gave your father the drug that knocked him out?"

"One of the men in the ambulance. Then he dashed back and got in so they could drive over and pick my father up."

"And where did you go when you checked out of the hotel?"

"I flew to Frankfurt. You knew I was going to London — I told you the truth — so I got on the first plane with a free seat that wasn't going there. Then I took a train to Cologne, stayed with a friend from college, and went on to London to meet my husband. We had a lovely time," she said, smiling.

"I'm sure you must have. Who is Simon Kaplan?"

"Simon? He's a dear old man who's known Gary's family for years. Do you know him?"

"I met him in Jerusalem. I thought he was a friend of your family and he was trying to help solve your father's murder."

"He's good, isn't he? He didn't know everything that was going on, but he served his purpose."

"Are the diamonds from him?"

"I really don't know who the diamonds came from. Gary and I didn't tell each other everything. Are we done here? I have an appointment."

I told her I didn't think she would get to the appointment. Then I opened the door and let Detective McHugh in. He cuffed Judy, read her her rights, and led her downstairs. I took her key and locked the door for her. No use inviting a burglar in.

EPILOGUE

Jack came home one evening with several huge boxes and spent some time setting up the new computer. Eddie glowed. Within days I knew he would soon be the expert in the family, which was fine with me.

The case against Judy Silverman and Gary Helfer was built in two countries. Judy's husband hired one of the well-known criminal lawyers we've all heard about to defend his wife, and I expect she'll get off with a light sentence. But Gary Helfer won't. The second man in Israeli custody eventually identified Helfer also, and he will stand trial in Israel after he stands trial here for fraud. The check made out to Double Eagle was returned to the estate.

I have enjoyed wearing my wonderful beads and the beautiful cross made of silver and Roman glass and have received so many compliments that I wrote the artist a letter. Jack wears his religious medals on his new chain and I notice him fingering it sometimes. It's really beautiful.

Eddie says he wants to go back to Israel with Grandma and Grandpa and put some more of that great mud on him. The pictures are hilarious, a small black figure with eyes and little else. He took it to school and everyone got a good laugh.

Joshua and Rachel Davidson are planning a trip to New York in the new year, and we intend to take them around and show them a piece of our country. We're all very excited at the prospect. I have never had friends from another country before, and I feel my life is better because of it.

Much later the intifada began and then grew worse. We had really hoped to visit Israel again and spend more time touring, but the trouble put a halt to all that. We both hope and pray that the country will see peace very soon.

No one ever found or heard from Simon Kaplan again.

We hope you have enjoyed this Large Print book. Other Thorndike, Wheeler or Chivers Press Large Print books are available at your library or directly from the publishers.

For more information about current and upcoming titles, please call or write, without obligation, to:

Publisher
Thorndike Press
295 Kennedy Memorial Drive
Waterville, ME 04901
Tel. (800) 223-1244

Or visit our Web site at:
www.gale.com/thorndike
www.gale.com/wheeler

OR

Chivers Large Print
published by BBC Audiobooks Ltd
St James House, The Square
Lower Bristol Road
Bath BA2 3SB
England
Tel. +44(0) 800 136919
email: bbcaudiobooks@bbc.co.uk
www.bbcaudiobooks.co.uk

All our Large Print titles are designed for easy reading, and all our books are made to last.